CHOSEN

PSI MATES BOOK 1

LEIGH WYNDFIELD

Psi Mates #1: Chosen

by Leigh Wyndfield

Copyright 2025 by Love Potion Publishing LLC

Cover by Sweet n' Spicy Designs https://www.sweetnspicydesigns.com/

No AI was used to create this book. This book cannot be used to train AI.

ISBN (ebook): 978-1-953545-14-5

ISBN (print): 978-1-953545-16-9

First Edition

For Chris. This one is all for you after you suffered my late nights, early mornings, and general distraction as I tried to get a whole series written at once. You were right - I was taking on too much - but thanks for supporting me anyway.

PROLOGUE

The four sisters swept Azia's room for electronic listening devices, using their individual sweepers, then switched on a handheld silencer Bayle had stolen from the Institute's security force. They huddled within the small radius of protection on Azia's beautiful bright blue and orange rug. They each had their own suite of rooms in the rambling fortress that housed the Institute, but they weren't naïve enough to think that someone wasn't always recording them. They were experiments after all.

As the years passed, surveillance on them had waned, and Azia and her sisters were taking full advantage of their mother's inattention.

While they shared DNA and had grown up together, they looked nothing alike. The four of them had the same mother, but their fathers were all unknown figures who had given them their distinct features. Bayle, tall and blonde, Caden, willow thin with dull brown hair she always wore cut close to her skull, and the youngest Dru, a black-haired beauty with elfin features. Only Azia resembled their mother, small and curvy, with a mouth that tended to frown.

"All this secrecy is a little over the top, don't you think?" Dru asked, raising one eyebrow.

"For once, this is serious," Bayle said, frowning back at her.

Since Bayle was the least serious of all of them by far, the comment immediately sparked anxiety deep in Azia's heart.

While her sisters tended to bicker, over the years the lack of parental affection and guidance had forced them to depend on each other. The love Azia had for them went beyond normal sisterly bonds. The oldest at twenty-eight, she treated them as if they were her own children. From the beginning, when they slept together neglected in the nursery, she'd been the one to comfort them after their nightmares. She'd taught them to brush their hair, to read and write, and it had been her who'd helped them master their psi abilities, despite not having any of her own.

"Stop drawing it out and get on with it," Caden snapped. She didn't like surprises.

Azia had known the family secret from her earliest memories, but she'd put off telling her sisters for as long as she could, wanting them to feel normal for as long as possible. When she could no longer avoid it, she'd told them everything—or at least everything she knew. As they all slowly came into their abilities, she'd had to make peace with the fact that she was the only failed experiment of the group. Since most abilities didn't manifest until puberty, her mother, Xandra ElAtal, had had to wait a long time to find out Azia was a dud.

"I found this in mother's lab." Bayle drew out a real paper notebook from under her shirt.

Fear tingled along Azia's spine. "Bayle." They got away with so much because they didn't draw their mother's attention. Stealing one of her notebooks would be an offense their mother wouldn't take lightly, but Bayle's psi ability lent itself to thievery like flowers took to rain.

"I know, I know." She shook her head, trying to appear contrite, but not quite succeeding. "But I had to swipe it. You know I did." Her look pleaded for understanding.

Azia sighed and rubbed her eyes. Bayle was a thief and had been since the day she could walk, so Azia should abandon any attempt to change her. "We talked about this. Never from Mother." No matter how much Azia warned her, Bayle just didn't fear their mother, even knowing some of what the woman was capable of.

"It's been over a year. I had to break sometime."

"What's in it?" Caden asked, getting them back on track. Out of all of them, it was her belongings Bayle took the most. Caden had stopped complaining long ago. They all had. Loving Bayle took a level of patience beyond what most people could handle.

Bayle hugged the notebook to her chest and leaned close to whisper, "The details of our fathers."

They froze, staring at the notebook. Dru with longing and Azia and Caden with fear. Their mother had been clear. They weren't to know of their heritages. That would taint the results of the experiment.

But Bayle had always wanted to know. Always. From the moment Azia had told her what she knew about their mother's work, Bayle had begun to research where their DNA could have come from. *"It can't be that hard,"* she'd say. *"There are only so many races in the universes with known psi capabilities."*

"So where did we come from?" Caden asked with obvious dread.

"I'm not sure we should know. Mother doesn't want us

to." But even as Azia said this, she knew that, for the others, knowing would help them understand their abilities. Not knowing put them at a huge disadvantage. It would be so much easier to understand what they were capable of, instead of stumbling around in the dark trying to guess or doing something dangerous by accident.

"Azia," Bayle said, ignoring Azia's warning. "Is part Delphi."

For a moment, Azia felt a spurt of excitement. The Delphi were one of the wealthiest and most sophisticated races, with high standing on the Interworld Council. They used their wealth to keep their environment naturally beautiful despite the fact their money came from the ore they mined beneath their planet's surface. To be one of them, to fit in and have people like her, would fulfill her greatest desire to not always feel so alone.

But the excitement was short lived as she realized they wouldn't want her either. She wouldn't have the abilities people whispered about. She was half of two things, and none of either. "That's impossible. I don't have any powers." Her mother had finally concluded that Azia's DNA mix was... too *human.*

"Delphi. Well, one of us had to be, didn't we?" Dru asked. Everyone knew about the Delphi since their planet was a primary source of the ore that powered space travel. They had one of the richest deposits and the mineral made them extremely wealthy.

"This means Azia has a mate," Bayle said in a teasing singsong.

"We all know I am the failed experiment," Azia said, brushing off the banter before it could take hold. She doubted she'd ever find someone to love since she'd long suspected she was missing a basic need for male—or female for that matter—company. She never felt curious, never had the same desire to explore sexually that Bayle and Dru seemed to struggle with. And even if she had a mate, a concept she found both abhorrent and somewhat thrilling, how would she ever meet them since they lived a universe away? As a rule, the Delphi rarely left their planet.

Dru, sitting to her right, gave her a side hug. "*You* didn't fail."

"And," Bayle said loudly to get their attention back on where she thought it belonged. "I'm Warfran. Whatever that is," she added, obviously disappointed she wasn't from a known psi race.

Caden snorted. "Whatever the Warfran are, they must be a planet full of thieves."

"True," Bayle said, seeming to like the idea there were more out there like her. She never seemed to feel guilty about her thieving. "And Dru is Morre."

"Who are they?" Dru ruffled through her hair with her fingers, a nervous gesture she'd had since childhood. Her raven locks sparked with a deep blue sheen when the light hit them just right, framing the flawless, milk-white skin on her elfin face. She was the smallest of them all, even though she could pack in double the calories.

"No clue," said Bayle, paging through the notebook. "But I'll find out."

"Bayle," Azia said, making her tone a warning.

"And Caden is Sargetti," Bayle finished quickly to ward off Azia's lecture.

"Sargetti. So, does that mean I can transform?" Caden's expression morphed from fear to curiosity.

"I think that might be a rumor," Bayle said. "I haven't found a single vid that shows a transformation. Don't you think in this day and age there would be?"

"I suppose."

They all fell silent, trying to digest the news.

Azia played with an orange tassel on the edge of the rug. It was odd to think she had a heritage beyond test tubes and artificial insemination. She hadn't had the same curiosity about her father that the others felt, because whatever abilities she might have had were washed away in the mingling of DNA, like blue eyes might be subverted by brown. The human in her had won out. But the fact she could identify the origin of her father hit her in the gut, and the secret longing she'd thought she'd vanquished built once again inside her. Pictures of family flashed in her mind, intimate gatherings she'd only seen in vids or read about in books. She'd always wanted that life so badly.

"I'm not sure any of this matters." Caden picked at the cuticle on her left thumb absently.

"Of course it does," Bayle said, a hard edge of outrage making the words sharp.

"The Delphi have blue-on-blue eyes." Azia pointed to her own white sclera. Hers weren't right. "This information may not be true." Besides, the Delphi were rumored to be able to detect lies, heal, and other things that no one else knew about because they kept their powers secret. None of which she could do. Her mother had waited until puberty, thinking that was the key. But her coming of age had come and gone with no psi manifestations. Then she'd performed a series of experiments to force Azia's abilities to blossom. Azia rubbed at the faded scars on the backs of her hands. She still didn't do well in dark, tight spaces.

Bayle paged through the notebook, running her finger along the harsh, cramped writing. "It's what she wrote in her own notes, so it has to be true. She wouldn't lie to herself."

Azia wasn't too sure about that. "Mother could have

planted the book for you to find." One experiment inside another. She wouldn't put it past her.

"Maybe. But this doesn't feel faked." Bayle's voice dropped an octave into their mother's deep alto. "Subject A...that's you, Azia...has not manifested any of the powers she should have displayed by this age, even allowing for the later puberty experienced by the Delphi. I'm afraid the increased human DNA mixture may have overridden the very Delphi attributes I wanted to highlight."

Azia had to agree that sounded like her mother. Xandra ElAtal had never hidden her disappointment.

"She's a bitch," Caden said, resting her hand on Azia's to stop her rubbing the scars. Only Caden had understood what Azia went through, since Bayle had been too caught up in her own oddities and Dru had been too little. "We should leave. Disappear. Poof! Then her precious experiment will really be a failure."

"She calls us Test Subjects A, B, C and D," Bayle went on, flipping through the pages, obviously having read every word already. Maybe multiple times. It had taken them three days to assemble, but Bayle had refused to even give a hint about her news. "Although, it's weird. There are pages missing where she's obviously ripped them out." She tapped the bottom of one page. "Places where the sentence is left hanging and then the next page starts in the middle of a different idea altogether."

"What does this bring us?" Besides more pain. Azia tried to keep her voice soft. Hurting Bayle wouldn't fix the deep hole in her own heart where a mother and father's love should have been.

Bayle looked up in surprise. "Answers. Don't you need them?"

"Not really." She knew exactly what her heritage was—a big fat nothing.

Bayle blinked incredulously. "Well, I need them. Don't any of you want to know how she got the sperm?"

"Not really." Caden didn't want to know, either. Azia wasn't sure if she really felt that way or if she was just supporting Azia's caution.

"Because we might have fathers," Bayle said, her heart in her eyes. "Real fathers who are alive."

They all fell silent. Real living fathers. Azia was sure her own father would be just as disappointed as her mother. After all, she was neither Delphi nor fully human, but rather some mixed mutt.

But to have a father might change everything. *Assuming Mother didn't kill them.* When it came to Xandra ElAtal, nothing could be ruled out.

"This is going to change things," Dru whispered, hope in every word. She particularly seemed to need what loving parents would have normally given her.

"And not for the better," Caden said, her tone full of the same misgiving Azia battled.

Watching Bayle flipping through the pages, reading scraps of their mother's notes aloud, Azia had a bad feeling that Bayle had finally stolen something which would come back to haunt them. Pandora's box had been opened.

Azia feared the four of them had just been released into the whirlwind of consequences.

1

Prison Planet 4132, three months later...

Prison Planet 4132, three months later...
The orders were a forgery, of course, but they were almost perfect. Almost, except for a small detail, which Azia didn't think the Commandant of Prison Planet 4132, known throughout the Interworld as Hell's Gate, would notice. But now, watching him study the paper so closely, holding it up to the light, she began to question her own hubris. How had she ever thought this would work? She hadn't even made it to the part of the plan where she went to Delphi and rescued Bayle from her current catastrophe.

Step one had been to find a Delphian who could sponsor her onto the planet. Caden had scoured every database and had only found one person from Delphi who could give them what they needed. Her sister was a genius when it came to information, so if there was another out there, she would have found them. Caden had spent her youth roaming around first the Institute's computer system, then the Troopers as a whole, then the Interworld Council's servers. She never did anything but look, which Azia suspected was why she was never caught, but Caden's curiosity knew no end.

There had to be a better way, but in the panic of the last two days, Azia hadn't been able to find one.

The Delphi did not mingle with other races. Living in close-knit communities on their home planet, they seldom left and rarely allowed others to visit. Somehow, her sister had not only gotten onto Delphi but had been arrested and charged with espionage. If convicted, the sentence was life in prison.

It had all started with that damn notebook Bayle had stolen. Bayle had been so intent on searching for their fathers, it was all she'd talked about for the last three months. Azia had no idea why she'd chosen to start with Azia's father instead of her own, but now Bayle needed rescuing from an impossible situation. Too bad the only sponsor Caden could find happened to be spending the rest of his life in Hell's Gate.

Locke Maynard wasn't just an every-day criminal, but a dangerous outlaw who had single-handedly killed an entire squadron of Troopers, stolen their ship, and led his pursuers on a nine day trip across the universes.

She took a deep breath to center her growing unease and immediately regretted it as the stink of Hell's Gate made her eyes water.

Hell's Gate was a prison planet made more secure because the only way to break out was to fly since deadly gas covered most of the surface of the planet. The stench had hit her when she walked from her transport to the main building, the sulfuric odor filling her extra-sensitive nose and making her gag. It became worse when she entered the building. Underlying the acid was the reek of unwashed bodies, urine, and the vague smell of human rot. She'd spent the short time she'd been here already carefully breathing through her mouth, trying to resist the urge to vomit or run screaming.

An advanced system of radar and surface-to-air-missiles protected the airspace around the planet. No one could leave or arrive without clearance from the Trooper's High Command. Clearance she'd forged. If the Commandant figured it out, he'd rat her out to her mother in a red-hot second. Then Xandra ElAtal would bring Azia in for questioning. Azia had never been able to withstand Xandra's interrogations. She'd end up telling everything that had happened, and Bayle would be in trouble, which might lead to a permanent end of her experiment. Azia wasn't going to let any of her sisters die, not on Delphi, and not at the Institute.

Commandant Schultz tapped his lips with one long finger and hummed, studying the forged signatures that were missing the correct stamp. Instead of the Office of Troopers, she'd only had access to the Institute's seal, and she could tell Schultz was debating if he wanted to call her on it. The Institute was its own beast within the Troopers and wielded an insane amount of power. She'd been sure Schultz wouldn't want to make any waves over it. Now, a bad feeling came over her. If she ended up getting caught, she had no doubt her mother would let her rot in prison rather than use her influence to free her eldest daughter. And Azia couldn't save Bayle sitting in a cell.

She reminded herself that she, Caden, and Dru had gone over and over their options. This had been the only plan they'd come up with that had a hope in hell of working.

Not that coming in here with forged papers, invoking the fear of her mother to get people to release Maynard to her, then leaving with him had been a good plan. It wasn't. In fact, it sucked.

But desperate times had called for desperate measures. She'd just have to brazen it out and hope Caden had been right when she said no one would dare question a stamp from the Institute.

"Is there a problem, Commandant?" she asked, using her mother's most impatient tone. The tone that always filled Azia with dread, even though she was twenty-eight years old.

"No, no, no problem," he said with boot-licking assurance. He stood behind his immaculate desk, ramrod straight, his black hair oiled, and his uniform spotless. His appearance screamed of order and exactness, a rule follower down to his meticulously polished shoes.

Relief flooded her. She'd been betting he wouldn't have enough experience with Institute travel orders to question the stamp. Those who worked at the Institute rarely traveled, focusing instead on developing the holy grail of the Troopers—the super soldier. The old fortress had the reputation for experiments that sparked horror to even the hardiest of souls. It was the place where rumors of hideous things originated, most of which Azia knew to be true.

"I'm sure you understand my time is limited. I need to meet with Locke Maynard now," she pushed. If the jig was up, she'd rather face that now.

"Of course, of course." He placed the paper on his otherwise empty desk, a strange lack of visible bureaucracy in the office of someone who ran one of the largest prison colonies in the universes. "I am only concerned for your safety, Captain ElAtal."

She snorted at that, then regretted the action as the resultant inhale brought a waft of foul air combined with

Chosen   13

the synthetic fish Schultz had eaten for lunch, making her stomach roll. "Let me worry about my safety." With an extreme act of will, she ignored the odors to concentrate. Time ticked away. She needed to get on Delphi and free Bayle before disaster struck.

Still, Schultz hesitated. "You won't be allowed to take in any weapons. With Maynard, we have a strict no weapon policy. Furthermore, no one approaches him without at least three guards. I can't stress enough the danger from this prisoner."

She bit her lip and considered his words. She'd been trained in hand-to-hand combat since the moment she could walk. Part of the experiment had been to evaluate their potential as elite soldiers for the Troopers, so she and her sisters had been given the best training money could buy. That didn't mean she couldn't be bested. She could. She just hadn't been in a long time.

"Take me to him, Commandant. After we speak, he may or may not be leaving with me. But I will talk to him alone."

Seeing how visibly wary Schultz was of Maynard, she wondered if it would be better if Maynard turned her down. She'd only been worried about the stamp, but now she realized the holes in this plan were deeper and more plentiful than she'd feared.

"You're removing him from Hell's Gate?" The hope in the man's voice had a bit more dread snaking through her.

She almost turned on her heel and strode back to her ship. Almost. If she had even one other viable option...

Technically, she did. She could tell their mother and have Xandra ElAtal sort all this out.

It would be tempting if Azia didn't know what their mother was capable of.

There had once been five of them, but Azia was pretty

sure Bayle, Caden, and Dru were too young to remember their loss. Riley had lashed out one day, using her powers to fight her handlers in a showdown that had left Azia, her mother and three others in the med-bay. After she'd healed, Azia had returned to the nursery but had never seen Riley again. It was one of Azia's earliest memories, the first time she'd had a friend, and the first time she'd lost one. Sometimes, she'd wake up from a dream, still hearing her mother ordering Riley to be *put down*.

There was a remote possibility the wording had been part of a nightmare, a delusion brought on by the stress and trauma. Maybe. But she knew Riley had been real, even though the one time she'd asked where the other girl had gone, her mother had claimed she didn't know who Azia was talking about.

Azia stuffed away those old fears and refocused on the present. She wasn't leaving. She couldn't. Bayle needed her.

"There is a possibility he'll leave with me," she said. After all, she had something Locke Maynard desperately wanted. His freedom. Of course, she wasn't really planning to free him. A dangerous criminal like him deserved a lifetime in Hell's Gate, but he wouldn't know she had no plans to release him. The premeditated double cross had guilt nipping at her, but her family came before anything else. "I'll be returning him after we're through."

He straightened into military posture. "May I speak freely?"

"Go ahead," she said, not looking forward to whatever was coming.

"I couldn't, in good conscience, send you in alone with him. He's dangerous."

The last thing she needed was anyone hearing what she had to say. She couldn't risk recordings or eavesdropping.

"I'm afraid that's impossible. Whatever happens, you won't be held responsible."

She could tell she'd said the magic words. The Commandant turned on a booted heel and went to the door. "Bring Locke Maynard to Interview Room One," he ordered. "If you'll come with me, Captain," he said, waving a hand for her to follow.

After passing a wand over her to check her for weapons, the Commandant hadn't spoken again, clearly giving up his quest to dissuade her. They stared into the empty room, a three-meter square dreary space with only a scarred table with a metal hasp in the middle and three sturdy chairs. For now, she stood at what amounted to a one-way mirror.

It seemed to take a long time for Maynard to arrive. While she waited, she reviewed her non-existent options for another way to access Delphi. She couldn't land on the planet without a sponsor, and she couldn't obtain one through normal diplomatic channels. Bayle must have snuck on using the thieving skills that allowed her to slip into locked rooms and off-limits spaces, possibly riding in on one of the diplomatic transports. Azia had always wondered if Bayle could become invisible. Although, if she'd been invisible, how had she been caught?

The door on the other side of the glass opened and three men dragged the prisoner in by a strap around his neck. They forced him into a chair, which must have been bolted to the floor because it didn't move as he struggled. Then they chained his arms down with practiced motions, carefully working at angles which would keep Maynard from laying a hand on them. It made the men's bodies contort oddly, but when the guard on the left failed to maintain the proper distance, Maynard managed to land a quick head butt to his chin. The guard snapped the left arm shackle in place just as he staggered backwards, grabbing his face.

The other two guards jumped away as one. Maynard sat still in his chair, his cold, calculating gaze on the mirror. He stared right at her, not that he could know it.

Azia shivered at his intensity. "Is that really necessary, Commandant?" she asked, trying to keep her tone dry and unemotional.

"I warned you, Captain. This man is dangerous. The Interworld Council should have terminated him instead of housing him in a prison. There is nothing about him that can be reformed."

Locke Maynard continued to stare at her through the one-way mirror. Chills raced down her neck at the stark fury in his eyes.

He can't see me. There is no way he knows I'm here.

But his blue-on-blue gaze pierced straight into hers.

They'd beaten him. There were bruises all over his chest and red welts crisscrossed his shoulders over older, faded scars, visible through the ruin of his ripped shirt. His hair, shaved close to his scalp, was dark blond, and the stark haircut accentuated his frightening appearance. He was a massive man, muscles on top of muscles, held in the rigid outline of fury.

She sighed. For once, why couldn't things be easy?

"Surely you see the necessity of not going in alone?" the Commandant pressed, his voice smug. He'd obviously been waiting for this display to try again to discourage her.

She could simply turn around and go home. Tell Dru and Caden that she couldn't convince Maynard. No one would ever know the truth.

Except her.

And Bayle, who would rot in prison on Delphi.

That's not going to happen.

"Tell your men to leave," she ordered, nerves racing through her despite her hard tone.

He shook his head. "Your mother is going to have my head on a pike if you get hurt."

Rumors of her mother's experiments were circulated in whispers around the Troopers. She was the monster in the closet, the devil under the bed. Azia had begun to suspect the things her mother had been accused of weren't nearly as bad as the reality of what she'd actually done.

"My mother demanded I come here," she lied, finally resorting to invoking her mother's name out of desperation. "Do you think I would dare to not follow her orders?"

His eyes flared wide at the thought of ignoring a direct order from Xandra ElAtal. "Of course not. This way." He opened the door, his face grim. They passed through the hall and for a single moment, he stood outside the interview room as if he had to force himself to open it. When he did, it was in a rush. The Commandant didn't enter.

"Ah, Schultz, I thought we'd reached an agreement," Locke Maynard said, his voice like warm honey mixed with danger, so much lower and more cultured than she'd expected from the brutish man chained to the chair.

Azia swallowed at the sweet-but-deadly tone and wondered what agreement the Commandant had reached with him.

"You three are dismissed. Please wait in the hall," Schultz told his men, then turned to her, not liking it one bit, but following orders like the good soldier he was. "If you're certain?" he asked, giving her one last chance.

"I am," she said, wishing her voice wasn't quite so thin. She suspected showing weakness to Locke Maynard would get her killed. She stepped into the room, picturing her sister in a Delphi prison, needing her.

"I've recorded our conversation," Schultz said, but what he really meant was *my ass is covered, it's your funeral.*

The four men filed out and shut the door behind them. The bolt rammed home with a snap, locking her in.

She stood frozen for a moment, knowing she'd crossed a line from which she could no longer return. Stupidity could get her killed. Dead people didn't rescue their sisters.

She'd cast the dice, now she had to brazen it out.

She turned to find Locke Maynard studying her closely, keen intelligence in his gaze. A cut above one eye had stopped bleeding, but inflammation had swelled it closed. She felt some emotion she couldn't name and realized it was pity. Like a princess who patted the head of a dragon right before it ate her.

Showing weakness wouldn't get her what she wanted, so she tried to calm her nerves as she sat in the chair across the table, scrambling to remember her carefully prepared pitch. She wanted him to come with her willingly, with as little fuss as possible.

He opened his mouth.

She held a finger up to silence him.

He raised the eyebrow of his non-injured eye, but remained silent, an annoyed smirk stretching full, masculine lips. His uninjured eye was the blue-on-blue of the Delphi, and he scrutinized her as closely as she studied him.

She took a small black box from her pocket and placed it between them, then tapped it twice. It beeped to signal that a field had risen around them so no one else could listen in.

"Nice," he said, his voice smooth and dangerous as he looked admiringly at the box, obviously recognizing that she'd just put them in an impenetrable circle of silence. "I bet Schultz is furious he can't eavesdrop." The thought brought him joy, lightening his features with an almost boyish jubilance. Harsh lines dropped away and his face smoothed into rugged handsomeness she hadn't been expecting.

The change brought her up short and she sat blinking at him in surprise.

He gave her a lazy smile. "Did you come all the way here to stare stupidly at me?" He glanced at the insignia on her uniform. "Captain—" He paused to let her fill in her name.

"ElAtal," she supplied without thinking.

His eye widened in surprise. "Surely a woman as beautiful as you is not related to the Butcher?"

She ignored the flattery as she winced at her mother's nickname. "The universes are filled with ElAtal's who aren't related to her."

"Nice evasion," he said, showing how fast his mind worked. Locke Maynard was full of surprises.

She wasn't about to go down the road where she ended up defending her mother to a murderer. "I have a proposition for you."

"Ah, here we go." He sat back and waved one hand. The cuffs locking him to the chair made a clink as he rapidly hit the end of the chain.

She wished she could stand up and walk away before she made a deal with this devil. "Help me get someone off Delphi and I'll grant you your freedom."

"An Interworld pardon?" he asked, not seeming as excited about it as she'd expected.

"Full pardon, to be executed after the rescue."

His deep, full belly laugh triggered an odd thrill in her stomach.

She tapped the table with a finger as she waited him out, annoyance nipping at her.

He sobered, finally. "You're lying."

Since she was, her nerves quivered. There was no way he could know that, though. "I'm not."

"You are." He narrowed his eyes as he leaned toward her, sniffing the air. "I can smell it."

Annoyed, she took a deep breath to reset her nerves and accidentally inhaled through her nose. Instead of the rotting garbage she expected, cinnamon filled her nostrils, the scent so deeply complex, she inhaled again just for the pleasure of it. She knew immediately it came from the man across from her, his scent curling through her and brushing against her insides as if he touched her. For the first time in her life, she wanted to lean toward a man instead of away, inhale along the curve of his neck where she knew the smell would be the richest.

He'd bite the nose off my face if I got that close.

The thought had every one of her instincts yelling *run!* Her nerve finally broke and she stood.

2

"Now don't leave," Locke purred, trying to calm her back into sitting. He hadn't meant to frighten her off, but his manners had grown rusty. "There's no reason we can't come to terms."

He knew exactly what was standing across from him in this hellhole of a room on this hellhole of a planet. A Delphi female. Not full-breed, that much he could tell. But half for sure. He could smell her, even over the foul stench of Hell's Gate.

She didn't look much like the women from his planet. They were tall and slim. This woman was short and curvy. And while she had the blue-blue irises of his people, around them was the whites of an Earth-Worlder, instead of the deep, deep azure of his people.

He ached to touch her, to invoke the ritual to see if this was his long hoped-for mate, even as he knew there was only a small chance that could be possible. Although, how many unmated Delphi females were running around the universes?

As a Delphian, he'd known since childhood that he had

a mate, a precious woman who was destined to be his. Part of his early adulthood should have been focused on finding her and invoking the ritual which would show they were meant for one another. His red flame would twine with hers, and the melding would turn their flames blue, binding them together forever. Instead, his search had yielded nothing, so he'd left Delphi on a quest that had eventually landed him in Hell's Gate.

His hands remained chained to the chair and his psi fighting powers were locked away in a place where only his mate would be able to release them. If he were mated, he'd be strong, he knew. Possibly in the elite class of fighters known as the Delphati. But instead, here he sat in an Interworld jail on a stinking planet, with no mate and no freedom. Lately, his interest in planning an escape had faded and he'd tried to come to terms with the fact that he was rapidly losing hope that he'd ever find what he'd come looking for.

Just when he'd begun to lose his will to fight, in walked this woman seemingly from out of the ether, with the keys to his escape.

Surprisingly, she didn't bolt, although he could tell she wanted to. He tried to keep his features relaxed and friendly. Based on the small jolt of concern that crossed her expressive face, he failed.

After a long moment, she returned to her chair. Her face, which had nowhere to hide since she'd twisted her brown hair back into a severe bun, flitted through a range of emotions he could read as if he were inside her head—fear, anger, determination.

No pardon was forthcoming. That much he knew. Not that he cared. If she took him off Hell's Gate, his options were boundless. He could steal a ship and run, slip back onto Delphi. Simply disappear somewhere the Interworld couldn't trace him. Safely hidden on the one place they could never give chase.

Watching her intently, he realized that even if this woman wasn't his mate, he could take her with him. Help her find her mate if he wasn't hers. Did half-breeds have mates? Surely they did. A half-Delphi was such an anomaly, he knew nothing about them except that a woman her age traveling around unmated deeply disturbed him.

"I don't need a pardon. If I help you, I simply need you to leave me behind on my planet." He attempted a harmless smile.

She inched back, then caught herself and gripped the table.

He'd never been a charmer, and there was a chance she could hear the duplicity in his voice just as he had heard it in hers. Although, he wasn't technically lying. As a people, the Delphi were good at prevaricating.

A plan coalesced in his mind. If she somehow managed his release, he would bring her to Delphi where she'd end up properly mated and safely tucked away with their people. She might not know it, but it was the best thing for her. She would thank him eventually. And if it turned out she was his mate, well then, he'd have her safe and sound with him. By completing the mating ritual, he would finally gain strength and realize his suppressed powers. With that, he'd become part of the elite Delphati fighters, a goal he'd always known he'd achieve if he could just find the other half of his soul.

He needed to calm her fears and leave with her, because staying in Hell's Gate wasn't an option. He would die before he'd come back here.

Her obvious desperation to get onto Delphi worked in

his favor. The fact his people had a natural attraction to one another, that as an outsider she might not understand, worked against her but was another weapon in his arsenal.

For a moment, he felt sorry for her. She must be terribly lonely. Delphians valued family above all things and spent a lot of time touching for comfort. It wasn't a sexual thing. They just needed contact with each other. He missed it. About the only human contact he'd had lately involved beatings—his and other people's.

"I can leave you on your planet," she lied again, her voice suspicious as she sensed the trap. "With some conditions, of course."

"Of course." He lowered his voice again and kept his face friendly. Well, he *attempted* to keep his face hospitable. It was hard to do with one eye swollen shut, but he had no resources left to heal it. "Then we have a deal? I'll help you free this person, and you leave me on my planet."

"I'm afraid it's not that easy." Definitely not dumb. "I'll require you to wear one of these." She produced a cuff from her pocket, holding it so the people behind her on the other side of the mirror couldn't see.

He knew exactly what it was. "Afraid I'll run?"

"Hedging my bets."

"Who wears the other cuff?" He tried to sound harsh and succeeded. If she knew he secretly wanted to be attached to her, she would be gone so fast, there would be nothing left but her chair rocking with the violence of her departure.

The cuff system was built so two people each wore one of the bracelets. If one person got out of range of the other, the cuffs would explode, killing them both. He'd worn a cuff before on his way to Hell's Gate. He'd been so pissed, he'd almost walked out of range on purpose.

He hadn't, of course. Because if he lived he might someday find his mate. His family's wise woman had told him she was alive but wasn't on Delphi. That's why he was out here in the universes, to find her, but his search had been expensive. He'd supplemented his income with black market trading. Which had, in turn, ended with him locked in Hell's Gate for killing the crew of a Trooper patrol ship who'd not only raided his illicit cache of weapons, but then tried to kill him. He should have turned around and gone home after it happened, but he'd stubbornly refused to go without his mate. Returning without her would mean that he'd never be the man he could be, never come into his power, never take his place in the elite fighting force. And he'd always be alone.

She raised her chin, but the fingers holding the cuff went white. "I wear it."

He fought the desire to grin, feeling lighter than he had in years. This woman, one of his kinsmen even if only in part, was going to walk him out of here. She was going to take him to his home planet. He tried to remain sober, tried to keep the mean look on his face. "What's the range?"

"Two hundred parsecs."

After four years in this hell hole, it was finally his birthday. "You first," he said, not wanting a double cross.

She took the other cuff from her pocket, holding it in her hand for a moment, the two cuffs lighting blue as they were touched together, signaling their match. She hesitated, and for a moment, his stomach twisted in panic.

He'd need to push just a little. "Who are we rescuing?"

She sighed. "Someone dear to me." That reminder had her snapping on the cuff.

A bad feeling came over him. What if she was asking

him to help rescue her mate? Rage flashed through him at the thought she might already be taken.

He calmed enough to sniff the air. Not mated. She would smell differently if she were. He jangled the chains that kept him locked to the chair. "I'm afraid you'll have to do the honors."

That gave her pause. She wasn't dumb, just desperate. Whomever she planned to rescue was lucky to have such loyalty.

She stood, taking a fortifying breath, then walked around the table.

He held his right palm open, wondering if he could touch her, then figured they would have at least several days to journey together to Delphi. Right now, his behavior needed to be above reproach, or she'd hightail it back to wherever she'd come from and leave him locked here, unable to find her again.

She stood away from him, reaching forward into his space, not knowing that he could have easily grabbed her, yanking her off balance, and toppling her straight into his lap, where she'd be at his mercy.

He remained motionless, inhaling her scent, enjoying the light cinnamon spice of her.

The cuff clicked in place with only the lightest brush of her fingers on his skin.

He could have howled with triumph, listening to the *beep beep beep* as it armed.

Commandant Schultz burst through the door, making Azia stumble away in surprise. "Stand back! I warned you he's dangerous."

"Too late," Maynard murmured for her ears only, satisfaction in every syllable.

Worry washed over her. She'd been stupid locking herself to this man. Why hadn't she seen the signs before she'd attached the cuff? Maynard's slow, triumphant grin had her reeling with the knowledge she'd fucked up somehow.

She had a sneaking suspicion that her carefully laid plans were quickly unraveling. She needed to escape so she could think. Locke Maynard had won; she just wasn't sure how yet. But she was a fighter, had in fact fought for herself and her sisters her whole life.

Forewarned was forearmed.

Maynard hadn't beaten her yet.

She slapped on her command face and stepped toward Schultz. "Unlock him. He'll be leaving with me now."

"I must protest." Schultz was winding himself up to be a

problem, making her refocus on the fact this step in the plan wasn't complete.

"The key," she ordered, holding out her hand for it. Her mother bullied people into compliance, and it had always worked. Azia reached for those lessons now. With the cuff on, she'd made her bed and would lie on it.

Schultz paused and she thought he'd refuse, then he turned to one of his men and nodded. "Give her the key." After it was turned over to her, he added, "He'll kill you." The Commandant had no doubt he spoke the truth.

For some reason, she didn't think Locke would murder her. She wasn't naïve enough to think he wouldn't kill, she just didn't feel he would kill *her*. At least not yet, and certainly not with the cuffs active on them. Her death would lead to his. Plus, he needed her to get him off Hell's Gate.

Cautiously, she moved into Maynard's space and unlocked his right wrist, every inch of her body quivering with suppressed nerves. The scent of cinnamon was a distraction she could do without. Then she placed the key on the desk before him and moved several feet away, figuring he could unlock the rest himself.

Two of Schultz's men held stun sticks, and based on their grim expressions, they were ready to use them.

Behind her, Maynard unlocked his left wrist, then one leg, his actions slow and almost lazy, as if he enjoyed drawing out his exit. Tension in the room swirled and lapped against her skin in ever-heightening waves.

She should demand he stop screwing around. They needed to leave before Schultz changed his mind and sent a message to her mother protesting her stupidity. Needing to keep focused, she picked up the black box and returned it to her pocket, drawing Schultz's narrow-eyed gaze. He'd searched her for weapons on the way in but hadn't found the silencer.

Finally, the last manacle snapped open, the click loud in the small room.

"If you'll lead the way," she said to Schultz.

"My men will go last."

"Mr. Maynard won't do anything while we exit."

"If he does, I will use the ultimate force to subdue him," Schultz said with relish, as if he'd been waiting for an excuse to kill Maynard for years.

"I'm quite certain he'll follow orders." She was on the path to freeing Bayle now and would navigate it however she could. She'd have to be smarter than Locke Maynard. Bayle's life depended on it. Besides, the cuffs would explode if her heartbeat stopped, so he'd have to keep her alive at least.

She glanced over her shoulder as Maynard climbed to his feet—up, up, up—*so massive*. He ranged above everyone else in the room. She was short compared to her sisters, but beside this man, she was positively tiny. He pocketed the key with a sneer. He was not only tall, but wide and covered in muscle.

I've made a deal with a devil. A huge, massive devil. I'm an idiot. And yet, she had to admire the amazing specimen of man standing before her, straight and proud. She had an odd desire to run her hand across the bruises on his chest to soothe him.

Shaking her head at her own stupidity, she followed Schultz as he marched through the door, one of his men at his back.

"You next," she ordered Maynard, not liking the mood of the two remaining guards.

"You planning to protect my back, sweetness?" he asked in that low, deep murmur meant only for her.

She shivered at the verbal caress.

Thankfully, he didn't see it because he'd already exited, tossing over his shoulder, "Does this mean we're dating, Captain?"

"Try to keep your mouth shut until we get off the planet," she hissed, suddenly sick of worrying about what she'd gotten herself into. "I need you moving on your own and you won't be if they hit you with stun sticks."

"Already territorial over my body," he said, so cheery she had to restrain her almost visceral need to trip him.

She concentrated on getting them through a series of four locked doors, every fiber of her taut with the stress of leaving with Maynard and the risk that they would somehow not be able to leave after all. Nerves hummed as she waited for someone to run out to stop them at the last second.

Schultz halted at the edge of the landing platform. "Good luck, Captain," he said, as if he knew she wasn't long for this world.

"Thank you." She strode to her transport, feeling eyes watching as she went, keeping her pace steady when she wanted to run.

Maynard dropped back to walk at her side up the ramp and she didn't protest, just increased her pace to the edge of a jog. He was so tall, he didn't need to lengthen his stride to keep up.

Instead of pausing at the top of the ramp, she kept going, leading him straight into one of the two bedrooms without giving her intentions away.

He followed her, as she'd hoped. She needed to lock him down as fast as possible and get off planet.

"You'll stay here," she said, waving at the bed and small desk under the vid screen on the far wall.

He glanced around at the basic space, not quite as far into the room as she needed.

To sweeten the deal, she tapped the vid screen to wake it. "Feel free to amuse yourself while I get us airborne." She knew someone who had been without tech for so long would be drawn to it like a moth to the flame.

He drifted closer and she faded back out of his reach.

The minute his finger touched the screen, she stepped out of the door and closed it, locking him in with her command code.

"That was a nasty trick, Captain ElAtal," he said in a dryly amused voice from the other side, so close she could hear him clearly. Maybe he even touched the door, although she hadn't heard him move to follow her.

"I can't be looking over my shoulder all day. Speed is of the essence right now and I don't have time to deal with you."

That monkey off her back, she raced to the cockpit and input the takeoff instructions into the computer. So close to being away. So very close.

At her command, the ship lifted off and she set a speed that would break through the barrier of acidic gas, minimizing the risk of exposure.

As they flew, she brooded, picturing Schultz sitting at his empty desk, studying the orders, debating if he should check them with her mother's office. If he did, it would take time. Maybe a standard day or even more, depending on how long it took for her mother to get around to answering her messages. Xandra ElAtal often spent long hours, if not days, in the lab. That could work in Azia's favor.

After what seemed a short lifetime, they were far

enough away that she could sit back in her chair and breathe a sigh of relief. Part one of the plan was complete. She had Maynard, which meant she had a sponsor to get onto Delphi.

She shook her head at the naivety of not even considering how hard it would be to control Locke Maynard. Worry curled inside her. She couldn't keep him locked in his bedroom the whole trip.

Could she?

No. That wouldn't be right, no matter how tempting it was. If she wanted him to negotiate Bayle's release, she needed him working *with* her. That would take compromise.

But she had no doubt that when she let him out, she would be uncaging a lion. Or maybe a shark was a better description. She waffled back and forth, wondering which was a better description and finally settled on lion. There had been something feline about the way he moved, graceful and predatory.

If she were completely honest with herself, there was something about him that intrigued her. His intelligence, the purr in his voice, something... she'd been fascinated. Even now, she wanted to let him out of his room so she could study him at her leisure.

Smell him again, just to make sure it had really been his scent in the interrogation room.

The thought was unsettling. Danger and her passenger were best friends. She'd better not forget that.

She typed a quick note to her sisters on their secret communications channel saying only *we're off*. No need to be too descriptive. Their mother had never cracked their communications, but that didn't mean she wouldn't one day.

Then she input the coordinates for the jump gate to Delphi. Exhaustion streamed over her and she closed her eyes, collapsing back into the pilot's chair. The extreme acting job to free Maynard had left her so tired she could barely keep her eyes open. Her limbs were weighted with relief as well as the new worry of a bargain she knew she would regret. She tugged on the cuff around her wrist, wanting to deactivate it, but knowing it was the only way she had to control Maynard.

Snuggling backward into a less unpleasant position, she fell into a deep, much needed sleep.

LOCKE'S HANDS flew over the keyboard for the vid screen. He restarted the operating system in safe mode to get around the lock-down she'd implemented, so he could navigate the basic level of the system. He estimated he had perhaps as long as one standard week of travel to figure out how to undo her electronic barricades to the deeper levels. Not that he'd need that long. These kinds of systems were no match for him.

It took only seconds to check what ship he was on. The information scrolled up the screen:

Ship: The Nebula

Class: XL4003, lightweight speed

Assigned: The Institute

Locke sat back, tapping the chair arm, thinking. This ship model hadn't existed when he'd been taken prisoner. The XL3000 series had been new when he'd entered Hell's Gate. Surely four years wasn't long enough to develop a new generation of transport? That usually took decades. That meant that the XL4003 had come out long before a new model would be expected, but really, what did he know about space ship production?

The fact she piloted a brand-new ship meant several things. First, she was a good enough pilot or connected enough politically that she had access to a ship barely out of development. Normal captain-grade pilots wouldn't be flying something this shiny.

Perhaps she was a test pilot of some sort? He mulled that over. She had the balls for it. He could still smell her from when she'd leaned into his space to secure the bracelet on his wrist. That had to have scared her on a visceral level, but she'd charged ahead. That took courage, even if it hadn't been that bright.

He stroked the titanium metal which had heated to the same temperature as his body. The explosives hidden inside might kill him, but without a mate, his life wasn't worth much anyway.

The manacle could be the ultimate weapon to control Captain ElAtal. She'd attached herself to him, literally, and it gave him a large advantage. Using it against her seemed wrong, but he'd done a lot of wrong things since he'd left Delphi, and he was willing to do a lot more to survive.

He shoved aside those thoughts to concentrate on what the ship told him about his current situation. The light-weight speed designation meant the vessel wasn't designed for fighting, although he was sure it had guns for basic defense. Built to run from one location in the universes to another quickly, these kinds of ships were for human trans-port, usually for dignitaries. They'd make it to his home planet in the span of one jump, since Delphi was located in a star system with a jump gate, facing no danger points along the way.

He'd use the upcoming down time to heal and regain his

strength. Hell's Gate had been chipping away at the backbone of his body and his soul. He would reverse the damage as much as possible before he arrived home. Showing up weakened would only hurt his family's standing even more than it had been damaged when he hadn't found his mate.

He'd been an embarrassment for everyone when it had been revealed that he didn't have a mate on Delphi and his original plan had been not to return at all if he hadn't found her. Now, he'd return bringing an unmated woman with him. Perfectly reasonable that he'd come home under those circumstances.

He slouched back in the chair, coming to the conclusion that he'd rather live as an embarrassment than in Hell's Gate, if those were his options. *Even without a mate?* He pondered that for a long moment and realized that even though the Captain hadn't come close to completing the ritual to see if they were mated—hell, maybe she didn't even know there *was* a ritual—he was starting to feel territorial towards her. It was a worrying thought because a woman either was or was not his mate. There was no middle ground. Yet here he stood in it.

He studied the vid again. The ship's Institute assignment gave him pause. When he'd first been captured, he'd worried that he'd attract the notice of the Research and Experimentation section of the Troopers. It's why he'd lied about his heritage when he'd been arrested. His cover must be blown, because Captain ElAtal wanted access to Delphi and knew enough that she needed a sponsor to gain admission to the planet. Maybe he'd never fooled anyone to begin with. With a sickening wash of relief, he realized he'd dodged a bullet not ending up with the Butcher at the Institute. He'd heard stories about her. Not where he wanted to spend his prison time.

Longing to return home suddenly filled him. He took several deep breaths to control it.

Unless he'd gotten outrageously lucky, he'd have to wait until his next life to find his other half. Sadly, he'd never been a lucky man.

He needed to bide his time, grow stronger. Maybe heal the broken ribs he'd picked up earlier today when the guards had come to get him. At Hell's Gate, he'd had a firm policy of never letting anyone touch him without paying a price, no matter the injury to himself.

Along with healing, his number one goal was to find out if Captain ElAtal was his mate before they landed in Delphi. The pull toward her was compelling. She smelled right to him. How much of that was wishful thinking or the sheer joy of being near another one of his people, he didn't know.

More fiddling with the computer's operating system was met with a series of error messages that he didn't yet have the patience to work around. He stood to explore the room, finding the tiny bathroom behind the first panel he touched. He stepped into the cleanser without disrobing, hoping the processor would clean both his body and his tattered, faded-to-gray prison jumpsuit.

Air whisked around him, swirling a fine mist that soaked his skin, scrubbing him gently. He hit the button to repeat the process, having not had anything more than a chemical sponge bath since he'd arrived on a prison planet that had no water source. After three rounds, he felt better but the uniform was on its last legs, hanging in ribbons from his shoulders. He shed the battered syn-fiber and did an even deeper wash, enjoying the first real opportunity in four years, even if it was sonic spray and not real water he washed with.

When he stepped out, he could still catch a whiff of the

stink of Hell's Gate lingering on his skin. No, not his skin, but his hair and maybe his beard as well. He'd do almost anything to cut them off, but another round of looking didn't reveal any implements to accomplish the task.

He stared at his own reflection. Hell's Gate had transformed his face into harsh lines, thinning him out, and leaving him with an almost predatory appearance. Putting his jumpsuit back on, he debated ripping the shredded top off completely, since it was little more than a rag hanging from one shoulder, but decided against it, since he had no belt to hold up the lower half.

Then he resumed his exploration, combing through the room, taking a survey of every compartment. The lockers held several uniforms and abandoned accessories. He checked the tabs, revising his assessment the ship must be new. Numerous crews had used this transport, based on the different sizes. Nothing came close to fitting him, although he found a belt that buckled on the last hole, solving the issue of his pants falling from his hips at the wrong moment. Sadly, but not unexpectedly, there were no weapons.

He continued his search but found nothing else of interest.

"Please strap in, Mr. Maynard," ElAtal's voice said over the comm. "We're entering the gate."

"Locke," he corrected without much thought, knowing she could hear him.

"Please strap in, Locke."

"And you are?"

"Captain ElAtal."

A half-laugh escaped him. He pushed a button and a jump seat extracted from the wall. Strapping in, he closed his eyes. He hated jumping. It felt like free-falling off a cliff as the ship went weightless, but getting quickly from one galaxy to another meant they had to enter holes cut into the fabric of space called gates.

His stomach rebelled as they entered the slipstream between realities, the ship turning at every angle all at once. It would smooth out soon, once they entered the stream proper. But for now, he sweated and tried to breathe through the nausea. In his mind, he pictured his home planet, full of water and green and light. He could barely remember the rolling hills and the beauty of his planet. His people had been careful with their resources, only mining small areas, with strict controls to limit the impact to the environment. The Delphi worshiped nature.

He missed it badly. Leaving had been the right thing, he knew that, but once he returned home, he never wanted to leave Delphi again.

Even if she isn't your mate?

He couldn't leave if the Troopers were looking to put him back into Hell's Gate.

Not even for a mate?

He couldn't answer that question. Death might be better than being alone, but Hell's Gate was a living death.

When they finally leveled out, not a moment too soon as far as he was concerned, her voice came across the comm again. "We made it."

Relief was evident in her sighed-out words, which flowed through him, both soothing and bringing a longing in him that he had to clamp back before it took hold and made him do something foolish.

He unclipped and placed his head between his knees, trying to calm his stomach.

"I know the feeling," she said, obviously watching from a vid.

He should care, but he found he didn't. "You can't keep

me in here forever," he said conversationally, sucking air in and out to quiet the nausea, relaxing as his stomach settled.

"Yeah," she agreed with another sigh. "Too bad."

He huffed a laugh. "You already have me cuffed." He'd have to shower again. Sweat covered him, pulling the scent of Hell's Gate to the surface. He wondered if he'd ever get the stink off him completely.

"As if that would keep you contained. You've already been all through my systems."

"Saw that, did you?" He'd thought she'd been distracted working on the jump. It was a good warning that he'd have to be extra careful to hide his movements from her. That was unfortunate.

The door opened to his room, and she trained a blaster on him. "I need a promise from you that you won't try to take over this ship."

"I promise," he lied.

"You just lied," she said, clearly insulted.

He grinned at being caught, but noted she wasn't completely without Delphian powers. "You lied when you made the deal with me on Hell's Gate."

"I didn't." She paused, leaning against the door jam. "Well, I didn't lie when I agreed to set you free on Delphi."

He raised an eyebrow. "You weren't going to set me free if I didn't go to Delphi?"

She drew up to her full height. "You're dangerous. That would be the height of irresponsibility to release you in Interworld Council space."

He smiled again, his facial muscles tight with disuse. "But you'll release me on Delphi?"

"They're your people. I expect they're more than competent to deal with you. Unless you been exiled?" Worry made her frown.

"Not hardly. I left on a quest."

"A quest?" That appeared to pique her interest. "I didn't know the Delphi went on quests."

"They don't." He tried to curtail her curiosity. If he was right, and her knowledge of Delphi was close to zero, then his advantage over her was enormous. He hated to use her lack of knowledge against her, but really it was for the best for both of them. He ignored a nagging twinge of guilt.

"Did your quest involve smuggling?" Her blue eyes were the right color, the blue of Delphi sky. They were really quite pretty against the white background.

She'd read his file. Of course, she would have, but part of him wanted to protest that she shouldn't believe everything she read. Even if they were true.

He shrugged off the odd desire to justify himself. "Quests are expensive, sweetheart. You have to fund them somehow."

She frowned. "Zip it with the endearments, Maynard." Her irritation wafted toward him, brushing against his skin in an almost-caress.

"Don't like pet names?" Not wanting her to lock him back into his room, he sprawled back in the uncomfortable jump seat to better study her. It had been so long since he'd been around one of his own. *Four long years.* He forgot about how nice it was to feel the vibrations in the air, smell the emotion. "Maybe you should give me your name, then. And don't go with the Captain bit. You're not *my* Captain."

She narrowed her eyes, then shrugged. "Azia. Are you going to agree to my terms or not?"

"Terms being what again?"

"You will not attack me."

"Okay," he said.

"Okay what?" she asked.

"I won't attack you. And you will take me to Delphi."

"You're a criminal who could kill me and toss me out an airlock."

"We're attached if you haven't forgotten." He held up his wrist to show her and tried to appear harmless.

"True." She shook her head, clearly debating.

"You really don't have any other options," he pointed out helpfully.

"That's true, too."

"And you need me to get onto Delphi."

"Yeah," she said, but he could tell she wasn't happy. "That's probably as good as I'm going to get." She holstered her weapon. "I'm going to regret this, but it's agreed then." Without another word, she spun on one heel and departed.

It had happened so quickly, he sat stymied for a moment, staring at the open door. Then he rose and hurried after her. "How long 'til we come out of jump?"

"Four days." She groaned. "I hate jump space."

Who didn't? They would never be completely stable, the air around them slightly off, their balance skewed.

They entered a small galley with a single table and four chairs. She pressed buttons on one processor and pointed to the other. "Help yourself."

Giddy over the thought of real, synthesized food where he chose the flavoring, he scrolled from screen to screen, debating his choices. What had he missed the most? It had been so long since he'd chosen his own food, he'd forgotten what he truly loved. On Hell's Gate, they'd been fed nothing but unflavored, unappetizing protein mush. He'd eaten it to live, but it had drained him in a way he hadn't anticipated.

Her processor beeped and she took out a cup of what smelled like real coffee.

Coffee, yes. He scrolled until he found it.

Now to choose food. He resisted the urge to watch her choose her meal as she pressed buttons beside him. He had to gain his strength back, so he chose meat proteins and vegetables, spending another few moments choosing which kind even if they were all made out of the same synthetic paste.

When the processor delivered the plate, he joined her at the table. They didn't speak as he methodically ate through the whole serving, relishing every bite. It was heaven, but more importantly, his body needed the energy. He stared moodily at her as she picked at what could be real bird meat from the look of it. It smelled like heaven.

"Still hungry?" she asked as he scraped up the last bite on his plate.

He gave her a nod. "Mind if I get another?"

She waved her fork. "Help yourself."

He ordered what she had on her plate, since he'd been envious of her choice after he'd started eating his own. When it arrived, he returned to shoveling more calories into his depleted body. "Who are we going to rescue from Delphi?"

"My sister."

There were two of them with Delphian blood? He stopped the interest before it jumped onto his face, not wanting to give too much away, but his insides twisted with excitement.

After years of searching and all the time in Hell's Gate, he suddenly stumbled on not one, but two possibilities.

"How did she end up on the planet?"

And why would she be unable to leave? If she was Delphi, even part, they'd open their arms to her in welcome. Unless she was a spy for the Institute. If she was suspected of spying on them, the Cadre might simply jettison her straight off-world, or they might kill her.

Worry filled her expressive face. "I'm not completely sure."

Now that she sat across from him, he could study her better. Brown hair pulled back into the usual twist Trooper females wore. The large blue eyes, her best feature, above a straight nose, above full, kissable lips. At first glance, she'd seemed plain but now on closer inspection, he found her beautiful. He couldn't bring himself to look away.

"But you're positive she's there?" He shoveled in more food, his body weeping with joy. He'd almost given up hope, he realized. If she hadn't rescued him, it would have been only a matter of time before he would have been circling the drain of the Hell's Gate cesspool, much to Commandant Schultz's joy.

"All I know is she's on Delphi and has been arrested. But I can't access the planet unless I have someone sponsor me, or so I'm told." She looked to him for guidance.

"Those are the rules," he said cautiously, which wasn't lying per se, just dangerously close to it, since she would be able to visit the planet as a Delphian without a sponsor, even as a half-breed. "Guess at what she's doing, so I can better prepare our arguments and negotiations."

She didn't want to, her mouth pulled down into a frown of reluctance. "I think she's researching psi powers."

"Because she wants to explore her own abilities?" If they were raised off-world, how much would they know about their power? Perhaps nothing.

She laughed as if he'd said something funny. "My sister is very sure of her abilities. She's obsessed with psi powers."

"I see." Although he didn't. Psi powers were a part of normal life, at least they would be when he had the power to wield his. That made him lean toward the theory her sister had been caught as a spy for the Institute.

"How did you know my sister had psi abilities?"

"A guess." He shrugged, figuring that even as only part Delphian, her sister would have some abilities. "We'll have to petition the Cadre once we arrive to see what she's being held for then."

Azia leaned closer to him. "One way or another, she must be released. As quickly as possible. The last thing we want is some sort of Interworld incident."

"Is she that important?" Why wouldn't they both just come through the open door offered to everyone who was Delphi? *Because they don't know it's open?* he guessed, knowing at once that had to be the reason.

"Yes." Only one word and said with complete conviction.

He waited for her to elaborate, but when she didn't, he realized the ElAtal name might be all her sister needed to be considered high value if she was caught spying. "What about you? Are you curious about your psi powers?"

If Azia and her sister were related to Xandra ElAtal, and he believed they were since she hadn't denied it, he found it odd that Xandra would have ended up with a Delphi male. Relationships outside of mating happened, and while Xandra may have had a Delphi lover, two offspring would mean a long-term arrangement. That wasn't something most Delphi could stand, even if they knew their mate wasn't available to them in their current lifetime.

While it rarely happened that someone would end up without a mate, suicide was usually the answer rather than finding an unfulfilling relationship with another. Not that he couldn't find sexual release with a random stranger, but why would he want to when it was a shadow of what he'd feel with his mate? He'd had a few dalliances but found them distasteful and finally had stopped trying. He certainly wouldn't have stuck around for the time it would take for a woman to bear two children.

She sighed and looked resigned. "Since I don't have any powers, no."

That brought him up short. "None?"

He wasn't sure that was possible. Nor, based on the fact she'd caught him lying earlier, did he think it was true. But he knew she'd told the truth as she believed it. He could only detect a lie that was purposely told.

He'd never thought about the implications of being a half-breed. Would they have normal abilities of a full-blooded Delphi? Or would they be muted to mere shadows of what was possible? Could they have no power at all? And if Azia or her sister were his mate, would he care that she didn't have normal Delphi abilities? Questions swirled, but he chose to focus on proving her ability to feel a lie. "Ask me a question."

"What?"

"Just ask me something."

She gave an annoyed hum but asked, "Why did you fight Schultz's men when you knew you'd lose?"

"I have no reason," he lied. Because he most certainly did have a reason. Schultz paid dearly every time he got into Locke's personal space. Not just in hurt guards, but Locke had started two uprisings after Schultz had tried to retaliate by crushing Locke's spirit. After that, he and the Commandant worked out an arrangement where Schultz left him alone and the whole prison ran smoother.

She gave him an odd look.

"Did I lie to you?"

"I don't know you well enough to tell," she said cautiously.

He shook his head. "Don't fight it, just tell me your gut feeling."

"Yes, you lied. But I could guess you did since it makes sense you had a reason."

He shrugged a shoulder to concede the point. "Do you usually find you can catch people in a lie?" Could it be she just ignored her powers? That she'd spent her life not even appreciating what she had?

She tapped the table with one finger. "I always know when my sisters lie."

"You have more than one?"

"Three."

Gooseflesh rose on his arms. There were four of them. Four chances.

He wanted to lunge across the table and force her through the mating ritual and if it failed, find her siblings one by one to see if any were his mate. He gripped the table to remain seated, fighting the urge until it subsided.

Besides being completely against custom, he knew a lasting breach of trust would haunt him if his mate felt abused by him in any way. Being unkind, and in this case, downright rude to his mate or her family, would set him up for a lifetime of hardship. He'd been created to cherish the woman he'd been gifted, not force her against her will in any way.

A little voice whispered that as she'd been born off-world, she wouldn't know if he'd treated her badly.

It was tempting. So very tempting.

Here he was, acting as if Azia were his mate, but he really had no idea until the ritual was complete. However, for the first time in so many years, he had hope. He wasn't going to do anything to destroy things if it turned out she was his.

He had time to entice her into the ritual. There was no doubt he could get her to submit voluntarily if he tried. She would want it as much as he, if she listened to her instincts. Perhaps he could simply talk her into placing her power into his hands. If she did it freely, then it wouldn't truly be coercion. Although, tricking her would be unchivalrous. Part of him, the part that had taken beating after beating in Hell's Gate, didn't care.

He put aside those thoughts for now and tried to get them back on surer footing. "Then you do know when at least some people lie."

"Well, how do you know if a stranger lies to you?"

"I feel the vibrations of the lie in the air."

She gasped out a laugh. "Feel vibrations?"

"You have red hair."

She rolled her eyes. "Of course, I know you lied about that."

"But the feeling of it." He growled, tired of her ignoring the truth. "Shut your eyes, stop laughing and concentrate."

"You know, don't you?" She met his gaze and held it, fear and worry and hope all mixed in her deep blue eyes which he could stare into forever.

For a moment, he was tempted to say *know what?* but then he decided that playing dumb would only draw this out and annoy her. "That you're part Delphi?"

She nodded.

"Yes." His heart thumped with longing. He didn't care that there were other sisters. *Let her be the one.*

4

He knows, Azia thought, shaking her head to deny it.

"I've known from the moment you walked into that room in Hell's Gate that you have Delphi blood." It was a statement, not a question.

A piece of her, one that always tried so hard to follow the rules, worried that she'd somehow revealed what her mother had always been very clear she must keep secret.

Fuck keeping it secret, she thought, suddenly angry. Azia was so sick of following the rules and being the perfect daughter to make up for her lack of powers. Besides, she hadn't told Locke that she was part Delphi, he'd guessed on his own, although how she didn't know. She hadn't done anything to reveal that she was part Delphi.

She didn't have the blue-on-blue eyes, but her pupil color was the same as his and the blue *was* different from normal humans. Searing and extra bright and vibrant. She knew when people met her, her eye color stood out most. The rest of her was average—brown hair, short stature, but not so short she drew attention, curvy body that wasn't too heavy but not thin either. Unlike Bayle or Dru, she could blend into the crowd. She was average, unnoticed as a rule. Not as good as Caden at fading into the background but good enough not to draw notice.

"How do you know?"

"That you're part Delphi?"

"My eyes—"

"Aren't double blue. True, although they are the right iris color. But your smell is right."

"My smell?" She resisted the urge to sniff herself.

"We have heightened olfactory senses. Haven't you noticed?"

Actually, she had. No one in her family could detect scents the way she could. She sat back in her chair, thinking of all the times her sisters had laughed at her for smelling things they couldn't. It had been a running joke between them. Even when she'd walked into Schultz' office, she'd smelled what he'd had for lunch over the general stench of the planet. She spent extra on food processors because the cheap syn-protein always had the vague scent of petroleum to her. Her sisters thought it a strange quirk. None of them, not even her, had ever considered that this could be a part of her unknown father's heritage.

Azia studied Locke, trying to figure out his angle. "You think I have Delphi powers?" she asked, because the question in her mind was why a man she'd rescued from Hell's Gate was suddenly offering her biggest desire.

He shrugged. "They go along with being one of us."

One of us. Being part of a whole, one of a group of people that automatically accepted her because she was one of them. The thought had her tripping mentally over instant feelings of hope and excitement, until she remembered that her mother had tested her over and over again and declared her a dud.

"You think I can feel lies better if I close my eyes?" she asked, catching on finally to why he wanted her to close them earlier. The practical part of her had no interest in this exercise, but there was a miniscule piece of her—that little bit that longed so much to not be a failure, that she'd thought she'd come to terms with so long ago—that wanted what he was offering, no matter how small.

"It might help with your concentration."

"Okay." She closed her eyes, feeling stupid but having no choice but to trust him, at least for the moment. "Now what."

"Ask me a question."

She was tempted to ask him if he had red hair, mimicking his earlier question, but then she realized she could ask what she really wanted to know. "How many powers do you have?"

"One," he said.

A whisper of *wrongness* floated across her skin and her eyes popped open. "You lied."

One piece of her brain went down the rabbit hole of wondering if she could feel only another Delphi's fabrications, but the other part of her brain was captured by the thought that he had more than one power. Curiosity flooded through her. Her whole life she'd wanted powers and this man might be able to help her find them.

He nodded. "And you knew it."

She closed her eyes again, not trusting the first try, worried she'd wanted it so badly, she'd made the whole thing up. "How many siblings do you have?"

"Two."

The odd whisper didn't come. "True?" she asked, unsure.

When she knew if her sisters were lying, she hadn't questioned it. She'd just figured she knew because she knew them. The same reason applied to when she knew her mother lied, although she had long ago realized that her mother did everything for the sake of science.

"Yes," he said, his voice low and purring.

A strange little flutter that had nothing to do with lying coursed through her. She ignored it. "Are you a thief?" she asked, since he went to Hell's Gate for stealing, as well a whole list of other charges.

"Well now, that depends on who you ask," he said, his voice filled with amusement.

She opened one eye and frowned at him.

He shrugged again and his grin widened. "Okay, okay, for the sake of the experiment."

She shut her eyes.

"I have never stolen another ship's cargo."

The whisper came again, like brushing her hair from the neck to the crown of her head. All wrong and uncomfortable, worse this time than the last. "Lie." She rubbed her arms to rid herself of the feeling.

"Nasty, isn't it?"

"Very." Although... she opened one eye. "Maybe you're just a bad liar."

He rolled one shoulder in a lazy shrug. "It's something all of us can do."

"Lie?" Disappointment niggled at her. She'd always been a terrible liar.

"Tell when someone is lying. Which is why most Delphi are very good at choosing their words to suit their own purposes. Rarely would anyone downright lie, since they'd be caught. You're starting to believe me." He sat back, waiting for her to agree.

"It seems I know if *you* do," she conceded. Then amended, "And my sisters." They could never get away with anything growing up. Especially Bayle and her constant thievery. Azia only had to ask her directly if she'd taken something and she knew the true answer, no matter how Bayle responded.

"No one else?" He raised an eyebrow drawing her attention to the fact his swollen eye was no longer shut. Still ringed in black but otherwise working.

"And my mother." She'd always known from the very beginning when her mother lied. Which was often. But the knowledge was not helpful since she never knew what the truth really was. Everything was hidden, secrets inside of secrets. She veered away from thinking about that. "Perhaps I suspect others."

He nodded. "It's easier to tell when a Delphi lies, because the vibrations are stronger."

She wasn't sure she felt vibrations. "I think my lack of full Delphi blood makes me different."

He rubbed a hand over his mouth, the action making his bicep bulge appealingly. "It's possible. Or perhaps you don't know what you have, because no one has shown you." He wasn't a classically handsome man, but she found her eyes constantly drawn to him. She could watch him all day, like a really good vid.

She forced herself to look away from his upper arm, fighting the urge to reach out and run a finger along the curve. "Maybe." she conceded, the thought so odd, she wasn't sure what to do with it. What if her powers didn't manifest, but were *learned*? Could it have been as simple as that? Maybe she hadn't been a failure after all but instead had simply been waiting for someone to come along and show her how. Hope she'd tried long ago to stomp out bloomed inside her chest.

"I could teach you."

She cut off the *yes* that automatically leapt to her lips, knowing he tempted her like the sirens of old. This man was a criminal. He'd ended up in one of the most notorious prisons in the universes for a list of transgressions that filled more than one page. He frightened the Hell's Gate guards to the point they sent three at a time to deal with him.

The fact she even considered letting him be her mentor was madness.

He offered her the thing she'd hoped and prayed for her whole adult life. Yes, she'd made peace with the fact she didn't have powers, but that didn't stop a large, hidden part of her from wishing she had them. She was a misfit even among a family of misfits. It made her feel always alone, to feel *other*.

"Teach me what exactly?" she heard herself ask when she should have responded with an emphatic no. Putting herself into his debt was a terrible idea. But hopefully, within the week, he'd be on Delphi and she would be returning home with Bayle. He would be the Delphi's problem. Although, for all she knew, he was an example of the male of the species. The thought gave her pause. A whole planet of hulking, muscle bound, trouble-with-a-capital-T males. It should make her want to run screaming but, instead, she had the odd desire to climb onto his lap and press her lips to his.

Whoa.

That was the most bizarre thought of her life. She did not lust and yet in the presence of this man, all her careful rules seemed to fly out the window.

He shifted, drawing her attention back to the discussion.

"A beginning lesson on Delphi powers in return for a set of hair clippers."

"Clippers?" Out of all the things she would have thought he'd ask, that wasn't it.

He ran a hand through his hair. "It still smells like Hell's Gate and needs to go."

"Done." She folded her arms. "But my lesson comes first." *Don't get your hopes up,* she warned herself. *This isn't the time to be crushed all over again.* What mattered was saving Bayle, not whatever she might discover in this galley.

"Your hand," he said, and there was something in his eyes that made her wary.

She didn't follow his directions. "Will it hurt?" she asked, remembering her mother's experiments. She wouldn't allow herself to go through something like that again.

"No."

She didn't think he lied but wasn't completely sure. It occurred to her that finding out beyond a shadow of a doubt if she were truly defective, truly a failure, would be painful.

Taking a deep breath, she placed her hand in his, ignoring her misgivings.

Awareness slithered up her arm, making her shiver, his touch like an electric current buzzing along her skin.

He tightened his hand when she tried to move away. "Don't you want to know?" he asked, his smooth, deep voice luring her.

"Yes," she said.

"Then relax. Nothing will happen if you fight your powers. Stress only keeps them dormant."

She tried to calm down. If stress suppressed her powers, it was no wonder her mother had never gotten anything to manifest. How ironic that her mother had used mental and physical pain, when according to Locke, that would make her problems worse, not better.

"Close your eyes again and think of a flame in the center of your palm."

She squeezed her eyes shut and tried to imagine it. But all she could feel was the warmth of his hand cradling hers, his skin rough with calluses. Yet his touch was gentle, light... respectful. Without her sight, the smell of him jumped to the forefront of her awareness, filling her nose, throat, stomach, all the way down past her belly. The spark of desire made her concentration slip.

"I don't..." she swallowed. "Don't think this is going to work." He was too distracting. Too big. Too dangerous. Too everything. And the feeling surging through her made her want to... she shied away from the thought of ripping her clothes off and begging him to take her to bed.

She met his blue-on-blue gaze, ready to bail on the whole experiment. She'd spent her life never being attracted to men, so she hadn't had any experience with them. Maybe this was normal when someone touched you and she just didn't know. Why did she have to find out *now*, with *this* man. Why not someone less... dangerous?

"Watch." He held up his other hand and a small, flame-shaped light appeared in his palm.

She blinked, completely distracted by the beauty of it. Red, with a rainbow shivering on the edges. Without thinking, she ran her hand through, wondering if it would burn and yet unable to keep from touching it. She was a moth to his flame.

There was no heat and no pain, but the action made him hiss, as if she'd done something to *him*.

But he didn't move away, didn't jerk his hand back or tell her to stop.

Emboldened, she slipped her hand atop his palm, so it was as if she held his flame. Her whole body burned and shivered, and she knew that she'd done an intimate thing, maybe even something forbidden. Desire sparked through every nerve ending. She held her breath, trying to suppress the need swimming in her blood. Her body, which had lain dormant for twenty-eight years, wept for him.

"Now add your flame to mine," he said, clearly not having the same reaction to her as she did to him, his face a blank mask, showing her nothing. "Close your eyes and concentrate."

Struggling, she shoved the desire away and tried to do as he asked. But even though she closed her eyes again, even though she felt energy thrum through her body, she had no flame to give him. Frustration warred with pure want.

She jerked her hand away and stumbled to her feet, her chair slamming into the floor behind her. "I have no flame," she said, trying to sound final. "If you want to come with me, I'll give you the clippers."

For a moment, he simply sat there, the blankness replaced by surprise as if he couldn't believe she'd give up so easily. Then he climbed slowly to his feet. "I felt some stirring of your power."

She'd thought she'd felt something as well, but she knew what it was—lust. She hadn't had anything like power inside her. Again. Like always. *You're a failure,* her mother's voice breezed in her ear.

Well, maybe when it came to power, but she'd rescue Bayle from whatever mess she'd gotten herself into. She wouldn't fail at that.

"Azia," he said, reaching for her.

She stepped back. "This way." As she led him to her cabin, she stuffed all the feelings back into the sad little box they'd lived in her whole adult life. Whatever just happened between them had nothing to do with power and everything to do with pure physical need. She might be able to tell if someone lied, and okay, she had a really good nose. But those weren't real powers. They were normal human abilities, just a little more, a little better. They didn't do her any good, really, if she thought about it.

What she'd felt when putting her hand in his was simple, base desire. Why after all this time she'd fallen for this man... a convict... she didn't know. She was defective in that area as well.

Grabbing the clippers, she slapped them into his palm. "Here," she said. Then, knowing it was dumb to leave him alone, she closed the door to her room, with him safely on the other side.

LOCKE STOOD for a moment with the clippers in his hand, then turned to stroll into the cockpit. He waited for Azia to join him for a bit, using the time to try to control the crazy wash of emotions swirling inside him. When she'd placed her hand under his flame, he'd almost hauled her across the table into his lap.

When she didn't arrive, he sat down and methodically combed through her systems. He wasn't looking for anything in particular, just poking around. Instead of answering the question of if she was his mate, all he'd learned was that he wanted her physically with a need so great, it almost had his control slipping. Luckily, she'd left before he'd done something stupid.

As he browsed, a communication popped up. *Read New Message?* with helpful Yes and No buttons.

He chose yes.

Is the Delphi cute?? Any chance your self-imposed chastity will end?

Locke leaned back in the captain's chair, which squeaked under his bulk. Chaste, was she? He found the idea appealed to him, although he wondered why. Delphi could have sex with others before undergoing the ritual, they just didn't often want to.

Although, what if she was his mate? Possessive need unfurled and grew. Azia could be *his* woman. Finally, he may have found her. Every fiber of his being had wanted to complete the ritual, had in fact *demanded* he complete it, but she'd run before he'd lost control. As if she'd instinctively known what he was doing, and she'd evaded him.

He knew it couldn't have been on purpose. She had no idea he was trying to lure her into the mating ritual. If he thought about it, his deceit was unchivalrous, so he pushed the thought away.

If she'd placed her flame in his, the mixing would have turned it the same blue as their eyes if she was his mate.

If. But she hadn't had a flame at all.

That brought him up short. His power hadn't rejected her, which gave him hope. Although, would it reject her even if she wasn't his mate if she didn't have a flame?

He was grasping at straws, and he knew it. If she'd placed a flame inside his and they weren't chosen, then the magic would repel. If they were mated, the two flames would entwine and change color. It was as simple as that. But she hadn't manifested a flame at all, so it was impossible to tell.

He wanted to believe his power had liked the feel of her. The sparking of need when she touched him had to mean *something*. Didn't it?

The thought was absurd. It was only the flame changing color that signaled a mate. No more, no less. He wanted her so badly he was imagining things.

Further complicating matters, he'd cheated by pushing her into something outside her understanding. A part of him felt bad for that. She hadn't offered her power to him voluntarily. He'd been tricking her into giving it to him. Not that she had. He hadn't even felt a return spark from her. He'd only told her he'd felt something so she'd try again.

Instead, she'd run.

But in this tiny ship, she couldn't run for long. Something lazy and dormant inside him he didn't even know he possessed uncurled and stretched. He promised himself that one way or another he'd have an answer. Soon.

She was skittish as a mouse about her power. Why? It made no sense. Powers were just a part of his race, were a piece of who they were. Fighting them seemed almost nonsensical.

Maybe as a half-breed, she simply couldn't call a flame. If that were true, would he want a mate who couldn't complete the ritual? To never be sealed to her? To never develop a bond with her? It would leave him as only a shadow of what he could be, since his own true powers wouldn't manifest unless her power called them forth.

Even with all those thoughts, a protective urge flew through him. Flame or no flame, a mate was a mate, and he should be happy to have her, accepting her no matter what. One thing Hell's Gate had taught him—there were worse things than not completing rituals or the lack of reaching his full power. He could be back in the pit. Instead, he had a chance to be with a woman he clearly wanted. That was something. Wasn't it?

He leaned back and shut his eyes. Just because her

powers didn't come the first time she'd attempted to call them didn't mean they would never arrive. If they were on Delphi, she could go to the temple to have a wise woman help her. He was a warrior, not a shaman. What did he know about manifesting powers? But even with his meager skills, surely he could do something.

He searched his memories for any stories of a Delphi not finding their powers. They had plenty of lore about finding one's mate and bonding. Plenty of stories even about death and the impact on the bond. But nothing came to mind about someone's flame not coming when called. It simply didn't happen. Or if it did, no one spoke of it.

He read the message again—*Is the Delphi cute?? Any chance your self-imposed chastity will end?*—before closing it, figuring he should leave before she caught him snooping.

Self-imposed chastity.

Desire stirred in him. He wouldn't want her if they weren't bonded, would he? Or had Hell's Gate broken him in some way?

He sat forward. What if she only needed a little help calling her power? Something to kindle the fire of her flame. Delphi's powers were heightened and expanded during intercourse. Energy fed energy and there was little in life that kindled a fire like intense, molten sex.

An idea came fully formed. He could lure her into bed, break her fast from men, see if her power manifested during sex. He sensed she had some power even without a bond. Sex might be what she needed to produce her flame. Need roared through his body, egging him on. If they slept together, he'd know if she was his, he was almost sure of it.

Too bad he didn't have more charm in his arsenal. He'd never had a way with females, but for the time they crossed jump space, her focus would be completely on him with them locked together on this ship. A frontal assault was needed. He could offer again to help her find what he could tell she desperately wanted. She might be upset at her failure, but she still wanted to release her powers. She'd enjoyed touching his flame. She had played in it, just for a moment, and he could tell she'd liked the feel of him.

For his part, the caress had felt like heaven. It had been all he could do to control his face so she wouldn't know how her touch made him crazy with need. If she had more Delphi knowledge, she would have smelled it, but she seemed determined to ignore her powers.

The thought of her touching his flame again decided him. One way or another, they would know. If he had to sleep with her to be sure, then he was willing to sacrifice himself to do it.

He buried the message from her sister below another screen and went to formulate a plan as he shaved.

5

The ship was small and Locke Maynard was a giant. Azia found herself tripping over him everywhere she went the next day. In the galley when she went to get her first cup of coffee, on her way back from the bathroom, when she sat in the cockpit doing her regular system checks. It seemed he was everywhere she needed to be.

"Don't you have anything else to do?" she asked as she shimmied past him in the tight hall when she was trying to repair the struggling reprocessing station, exasperated and overwhelmed. She'd never had a male in her personal space outside of basic training and she found her attraction to him annoying in the extreme. She couldn't seem to stop thinking about his flame in her cupped palm, the image remained in the forefront of her mind. She longed to hold it again, to see if it had simply been because of a new experience rather than the man himself.

"Actually, I don't." He gave her a slow, easy grin that made her want to take two steps backward. Or maybe two steps forward. Without the beard, his smile was even more appealing.

"You need a shirt," she said, grumpy about having to stare at his amazing abs peeking from the shredded jumpsuit for the second day. She dropped the tool she'd need beside the access hole she'd been working in for the last hour. There were several uniforms in her room. Maybe something would fit. And if it didn't, she'd cut a hole in a bed sheet and make him wear it like a poncho.

He trailed behind her. She couldn't hear his tread, which was silent, an incredible feat for such a big man, but she could feel him. As she had all day. Argh!

When she reached her cabin, he lounged in the doorway, not daring to come in, which was a pity because then she'd have the satisfaction of throwing him out. She opened the closet and flipped through the uniform shirts hanging there. There were leftover items from past crews stuffed in various places all over the ship.

While she was a Captain in the Troopers, once she'd completed basic training, she'd been assigned to her mother's staff at the Institute, in administration. She'd slowly worked her way up the ladder, taking the tests to advance each rank as they became available to her, until she'd ended up at her current rank. She knew she was at the end of the road. She couldn't go further in the hierarchy without combat experience, something her mother had forbidden. She and her sisters were all trained for combat and spy work, but except for Bayle, they hadn't had real world experience since her mother hadn't wanted them to leave her presence. Bayle's escape to do mission work had left Azia both envious about the taste of freedom and relieved that she didn't have to go.

Azia flipped through the spare uniforms quickly. No, no,

no. All too small. Then she stopped. Maybe. She pulled out an extra-large size, handing it to him, then quickly flipped through the rest. "It's this or nothing."

"Thanks." He held it up to his massive chest. "About your power..."

She tried to head him off. "It's non-existent."

He lowered his hand, letting the shirt hang by his side as he blocked the exit. "We both know that isn't true. You can tell if someone lies. You have extra olfactory senses of a Delphi."

"Those aren't powers." She'd worked it all out last night while she lain in bed reviewing the short lesson he'd given her. Extra scent detection came from a difference in nose structure. And if she really felt vibrations from a lie, which she wasn't completely sure she did, then that too would be a physical thing, totally unrelated to psi power. "Neither of those means I have true power."

"I would argue being a human lie detector *is* a power. Besides, I grew up playing with my flame from an early age. It was a children's toy to all of us. It never crossed my mind I wouldn't be able to control it because I just assumed I could. You missed that opportunity."

"Your point?" She'd gotten beyond all this. She'd moved on and was a functioning human being with a satisfactory life. It was annoying to drag this back up after she'd settled it in her mind.

"We can't give up after just one try."

"We?"

"I have a vested interest in this."

"No, you don't." That was absurd. Her power, or lack of it, had nothing to do with him.

"You will need to be as Delphi as possible when we

arrive to negotiate for your sister. I can't free your sister without your participation."

His blue-on-blue eyes appeared sincere and he hadn't lied, but she was sure he wasn't exactly telling the truth either. Although, what did it matter? The part of her that wanted powers, the part of her she'd thought she'd destroyed, had roared back in full force. Here was a Delphi in the flesh offering to teach her. The pain of failing again had her reluctant to move forward.

"The older you get, the harder it will be to learn," he added, his face sincere, but she wondered at his motives.

"If I need to be young to learn, that ship has sailed. Why do you care so much?" Although it made sense it would only become harder with the passage of time. Like learning a new language was easier for children, learning to wield her power might be easier as well.

"It pains me that you're missing such a big piece of yourself."

Truth, and yet—he was hiding something. But again, did it matter? She wanted to explore this piece of herself and now she had a chance. That didn't mean she trusted him completely, but why not take advantage of what he offered?

Internally, she sighed with exasperation over her indecision. Last night, she'd finally slept after accepting the fact she had no powers, now here she was jumping back into trying again. She was giving herself whiplash. "What do you propose?" she asked, unable to walk away.

"Daily lessons."

She didn't like the sound of that. It was too intimate. He was already starting to drive her crazy with his nearness. But how much did she want this? She had to admit... she wanted it badly.

"An hour every morning after breakfast, then you leave

me alone for the rest of the day," she said, trying to put a box around it.

He shook his head. "Don't cut the time short. We need a few hours at least."

"Two." She wasn't going to spend longer with him. He already took up too much space in her mind. "And only for the next two days. If there is no sign of my powers, then I'm pulling the plug."

He nodded, although from his expression, he was reluctant to agree. "We'll start there. When we make progress, you'll change your mind."

"The shirt goes on," she said, not willing to spend another moment looking at rippling abs under velvet-smooth skin.

He grinned. "Don't want to look at my fantastic stomach?" He placed a hand on his torso to draw her gaze there.

She stared at his perfect washboard, her palms itching with the need to touch. "No."

"Go ahead and lie to yourself. You can't lie to me," he said, laughing at her. "Let's go work in the galley, then."

"Give me twenty," she said, putting it off. She had to be an idiot to make this bargain.

But what if I find my power? Her childhood dream seemed to shimmer within her grasp.

It was worth a try. And try she would for the next two days. If she didn't make any progress by then, she'd give up and accept her fate. Again. The thought both exhausted her and gave her hope.

She stared at the vid screen next to her bed which showed the blur of space outside the ship, a streak of stars and blackness. Usually, she found it pretty but now she felt trapped and hunted. Which was stupid, she knew. In a few days, Locke Maynard would be off her ship, Bayle would be rescued, and Azia could go back to her old life. For some reason, the thought didn't appeal to her as it once had.

Using the extra time, she returned to finish the repairs to the reprocessing station, blessedly alone.

LOCKE WRACKED his brain for a way to help Azia find her flame. He'd never been taught himself, although he supposed he'd watched his brothers and his parents as he grew up. They'd provided the examples he'd needed to learn. He could provide an example for Azia.

He waited impatiently at the galley table for a couple seconds, then made himself a cup of coffee just for fun. He had a deep abiding love for her food processors. Tempted to make a snack, he scrolled through the options as he sipped. Already he could feel his strength returning, faster than he'd anticipated. He'd been worried his time in Hell's Gate had permanently impacted him, and while he was sure he'd never forget the horrors of it, he now knew that his body, at least, would recover. If he could bring his power up a little higher, he'd be able to heal the injury to his ribs that continued to bother him every time he turned the wrong way or took too deep a breath. He'd been able to get rid of the bruising on his torso and soothe the aching muscles there, as well as clear up all but the bruise around his eye.

Syn-potatoes, he decided.

Baked or fried? The computer queried.

Hmm... decisions. He chose fried.

Then he waited in anticipation as the machine whirred.

Behind him, Azia arrived. He felt her move through the room, the only sound the scraping of the chair as she sat.

"Are you hungry again?" she asked, amused.

"I'm making up for lost ground." He picked up his snack and sat in the seat closest to her, grinning as she stiffened and inched her chair away. "I'm hoping to gain enough power to heal my ribs."

Her eyes grew wide. "You can do that?"

"Every Delphi can to some degree." He took a big bite while she stared at him. Fried fake synthetic potato exploded in his mouth. Gods above, he could eat these for the rest of his life and never stop, it was so good.

For a moment, he just savored the food but finally pulled himself back to the matter at hand. "Powers can range in strength, but we all have the base abilities. I can heal myself but not others. It's possible to heal outside yourself if you're strong enough and skilled enough in that area."

As she took that in, he shoveled in the food. Fried anything was delicious.

"Maybe I won't have any level of skills."

Maybe she wouldn't. He had no way of knowing. "We already know you can smell more than full-blooded humans, and that you know when people lie to you." With sadness, he took the last heaping bite and then tossed the plate into the recycler.

She nodded, the action slow and hesitant.

"Which means you have at least some level of Delphi powers. It makes sense you might have others."

"Or I might not."

"Or you might not," he agreed, hoping that wasn't the case. Because even if she wasn't his mate, she'd be someone else's, so they had to figure this out. The thought that she might belong to another bothered him, but he shoved it away. "I have been thinking about how to teach you to call your flame. It's something Delphi do as children, but it occurred to me we watched those around us for examples.

Was your father not able to teach you?" If Xandra ElAtal was the mother, then her father must be the one with Delphi blood. Delphis had strong family clans and he wondered which one she belonged to.

"He wasn't there when I was growing up." She didn't lie, but he suspected she wasn't telling him the whole truth.

He didn't push what could be a sore subject, even though he wanted to very badly. "What about your sisters?"

"They have power, but they're younger than I am. By the time they started showing the signs, my mother already decided that I wasn't going to manifest any abilities."

Surely the mother goddess wouldn't be so cruel as to reveal four females that needed mates and have none of them be his? A growing part of him wanted only Azia, but he knew if she wasn't his, he would take any of the others and count himself lucky. "How old were you when your mother decided you had no abilities?"

"Sixteen."

"Young for a Delphi to come into their power. Besides, if your mother wasn't Delphi, why would she assume your powers would develop without training?"

She shrugged one shoulder. "It's just what she told me and I believed her." A tiny bit of hope peeped into her voice.

He rested his hand on the table near hers. "When I call my power, I think of it as a deep well inside me. I dip into that reserve and call my flame." He demonstrated by calling up a spark in his hand.

She stared at the red glow as if it would bite her. "I don't think I have a well inside me."

"Touch the flame," he said, holding his hand toward her, wondering if it would feel as good this time as it had previously. Touching another's power just wasn't done between adults. Sure, as children, he and his siblings had run their hands through each other's flames, playing games with them and learning control. But as a Delphi aged, they reserved that behavior for their mate only.

She tentatively ran one finger across his palm.

Pleasure burst within him. Did it feel good because it had been so long since he'd touched another Delphi? Or was it something more? He would only know if he completed the ritual by combining their flames and watching for the telltale shift to blue. He tried to think back to childhood. No memories of ever feeling pleasure came to him, so he didn't think it was only the act of someone touching his flame at work here.

Usually, a wise woman would reveal your mate to you, and the ritual would seal the two people together, confirming the choice. But he was out here in the middle of Interworld space and even though they would eventually arrive on Delphi, Locke wasn't willing to wait that long to know. If she was his mate, his life would be perfect. They would bond, move into his rooms in his family's compound and raise their children in the way of the Delphi. A small niggle of worry bit at him. Could he live a normal life after Hell's Gate?

Another wisp of worry filtered through him. Would Azia be happy living in the strict structure of the Delphi culture? Now that he'd been out in the universes, he wondered how well an off-worlder could adjust. In fact, he suspected *he* was going to struggle to fit back in the structure of his old life.

He'd been gone four years, in prison for most of that. During that time, he'd done whatever he'd felt like doing. He hadn't prayed to his ancestors as he was required to at home. He didn't have to constantly eat communal meals that could become tense with the stressors of many large personalities interacting constantly. He wasn't consigned to the status of the second son, with the obligations that he'd been raised to fulfill.

It suddenly occurred to him that if his wife was an off-worlder, she may not fit in with the expectation that a woman would quietly raise her children and remain largely hidden safely at home. This woman before him was a Captain in the Troopers. She'd wielded enough power to walk into Hell's Gate and demand Schultz hand him over. Could she fit neatly into the box Delphi women were expected to live in?

For a second, he tried to imagine this vibrant woman sitting meekly beside him at one of the almost constant holy day celebrations. He couldn't make the image coalesce in his mind.

He shoved those thoughts aside to focus on the here and now. "You're one of us. I knew the moment you walked into the interrogation room at Hell's Gate."

"Because of my smell," she said, a bit of disbelief in her voice.

"Right." He moved his palm, still cupping his flame, closer to her. "See if you can take the flame from my palm. Scoop it from my hand into yours." They'd done this as children, passed flames back and forth. One of his early memories was of playing like this with his older brother. Delphi struggled to have children and often only had one, but Locke had two brothers, one younger and one two years older than him. It had been an unusual childhood and made his extended family compound even more lively.

She cupped her hand and worked it under his flame.

He resisted the urge to shiver. "Picture yourself taking it from my hand as you move away."

It almost worked. The flame began moving with her. Then it slid back into the center of his palm once more.

"Close," he encouraged. "Try again." The feel of her hand cradling his power made desire spike hard and insistent inside him. He leaned toward her and inhaled her scent, drawing it deep in his lungs. Cinnamon and clean woman. He could smell her all day, every day, for the rest of his life.

She repeated the gesture, but this time the flame didn't move at all.

Desire built inside him with every attempt. A sheen of sweat broke out across his brow. He worked hard to ignore it. "What did you do the first time that you aren't doing now?"

"I have no idea."

"Think." It came out as more demanding than he'd meant it to, but he was fighting his desire and couldn't soften it in time.

"I don't know," she said, a note of annoyance in her voice.

He covered her hand with his, extinguishing his flame on her flesh, enjoying the touch of her, gentling his voice. "Don't get upset. It's harder to access your powers if you're stressed. It might be you're trying too hard." He brought back up his flame and rolled it from hand to hand, melding it into a ball.

She watched, clear longing in her face.

"Put your hand in between mine and let it roll across you," he said, clutching at straws.

The flame rolled from one hand to another without skipping her skin, but no matter what he did, he couldn't get it to stay on her hand. Frustration grew as he searched his childhood memories. How had it felt the first time he'd called the flame? What had happened? He had been ten when the flame came, but it had been expected and while exciting, it just showed up one day. Like a faucet that was one day off, then the next gushing on.

He slowed down the roll, leaning toward her, rocking it back and forth across her palm. Her breath panted and he realized he also gasped for air, desire so fierce inside him, he could barely breathe. They were so close... their foreheads were a hair's breadth apart. He could tip his head up and his lips would meet hers. He'd never wanted anything so much as he wanted to take her mouth with his.

For the briefest moment, his flame paused on her hand. "Oh," she gasped, her red lips rounded in surprise and excitement, her blue eyes shining with hope.

He kissed her, forgetting everything but his own desire.

After a second of stillness, her lips moved on his, opening to him, their tongues touching and exploring. She rested her hand on his shoulder as she leaned in, her fingers trembling.

Everything faded but the softness of her lips and the cinnamon flavor of her tongue filling his senses, spicy and sweet.

Then she pulled back, and he knew the moment when she realized what she was doing and rejected it. He let her retreat, knowing at least that the desire he felt so sharply wasn't one-sided. He had more time. They were still in deep space. They wouldn't exit for four days. Plenty of opportunity for him to make his move. He figured she would resist him, but their chemistry alone boded well for his chance to lure her closer.

He gave her a lazy smile and ran one finger across the back of her hand. "We would be good together, you know," he said, tempting her with the simplicity of touch.

Her hand jumped on the table, but she didn't move away. "I—"

He raised one eyebrow, waiting for her to get out the rest of her sentence but instead she looked at him helplessly. "Delphi have no issue having sex with one another before we're mated. You'll enjoy me." He leaned closer. "And I know I'll enjoy you."

Her scent wafted all around him, deeper and richer now with her desire. It was all he could do not to launch himself across the table, but he held still. This was about seduction. He had days to convince her, to plant the seed and let it grow. Rushing could end his chances completely.

Her breath sawed in and out as if she'd been running and her eyes were wide. Then she stumbled from her chair, not meeting his gaze. "I—I need to check the fix to the reprocessing station to see if everything is working properly."

"You should try again to call your power." He didn't want to give up, didn't want to let her go, but forcing her would only make him lose everything. "It rested on your palm. That's the first step."

"Tomorrow," she said before she hurried from the room, and left.

He sat back, resisting the urge to chase her. "Tomorrow," he murmured like a promise.

6

After the longest day of her life, Azia lay in bed
unable to sleep, her mind spinning with the feel
of Locke Maynard's flame and the possibilities of
her own power.

And the kiss they'd shared.

She closed her eyes and could feel the press of his lips
on hers, both hard and soft. A shiver of need raced over her,
as if he were kissing her again right then instead of hours
earlier. With a trembling hand, she brushed a finger across
her lips. Holy smokes. She would never forget that moment
if she lived to be a hundred. She could have lost herself in
his kiss forever. A part of her had wanted to do it. No, *needed*
to do it.

The rest of her didn't like the feeling of careening out of
control.

For the first time in her life, she desired another person.
After long suspecting she was defective in that area as well,
it was a tremendous relief. Adding to her pleasure, Locke
Maynard had fully participated in the kiss, had, in fact, initi-

ated it. It had literally curled her toes. Not bad for a first kiss. Not bad at all.

Bayle was always teasing her about her lack of interest in men. Perhaps she only had interest in Locke because he was Delphi? What if instead of being frigid, she was only attracted to people from her father's planet? Maybe there was something about his DNA that called to her.

Since she was never going to see another Delphi again after she freed her sister, the thought depressed her on a deep level. It wasn't that she didn't want what others had— love, marriage, children. It's just that she had made peace with the fact she wasn't going to have those things.

Lying in her lonely bed, her body burned for Locke. She wanted him. Of that she had no doubt at all. She could fall into bed with him and run her hands over all that sexy, hot muscle without a second of debate. She was certain he would welcome her.

When they arrived on Delphi and negotiated Bayle's release, her window of opportunity to explore all the things she'd heard about sex and intimacy, things that she'd come to accept weren't an option for her, would close. Locke would stay on his planet with his people, and she would return to the Institute. She'd come to terms with the life she lived, but now that she had a possibility of something more...

She stared at the ceiling in her cabin, watching the lights from the vid screen reflect and flicker. Usually the faint glow reassured her, but now she found Locke had taken away her inner peace.

She had someone on her ship who'd offered to be her bed partner and let her explore all the things she'd always wondered about. With no consequences. She could have him and cradle the memory.

So why was she hesitating? Why was she denying herself the only shot she might ever have to be with someone she desired? She acted as if she'd bought into all the things her mother had said in frustration and anger when the experiment had failed. Was she sabotaging herself?

She mulled that over for a long moment. Maybe, for once, she could be selfish.

Was it a bad idea to sleep with a convicted criminal? Of course it was. But perhaps being stupid was something she needed to do, since being smart had left her lonely.

If this was her only shot at enjoying sex—and that was a big if, because her hypothesis that she was only attracted to Delphi men seemed flimsy, especially since she'd only met one of them—then perhaps she should grab this opportunity with both hands. March into Locke's room and ask him if he wanted her.

Take off her shirt and slink toward him like a siren.

She covered her eyes with her hands despite lying in the dark. That was the most ridiculous idea she'd ever had.

You're an idiot.

Maybe. But being the peacemaker and always worrying about other's feelings had gotten her nowhere in life. Except alone.

Still unsure of her path, she threw off the blanket and padded barefoot to the kitchen to make herself a glass of syn-milk to help her sleep. In the dark room, lit only by the food processor's helpful glow, she pressed the buttons, asking for it to be heated, hoping that would do the trick. If she could fall into oblivion, she'd stop thinking about him.

"Can't sleep?" Locke's deep, honeyed voice asked in the darkness.

She jumped. "Nope," she said, since he'd know if she lied. She didn't turn to him as she waited for her beverage, afraid he'd see the desire on her face even in the weak light of the processor.

"Me either."

"Hmm," she said, not really knowing what to say to that. Perhaps he normally had insomnia and his lack of slumber had nothing to do with her.

She took a quick peek over her shoulder while her milk dispensed to find his dark form lounging in a nearby chair. She wanted to stride across to where he sat, straddle his lap, and explore the muscles clearly outlined in the vague light in the kitchen.

Behind her, a glass clinked on the table as he set it down. "I'm so turned on from our kiss earlier, I needed a shot of liquor to help me calm down."

He said it so dryly it took her a moment for the words to settle in her mind. When they hit her, she blinked in shock, taking a deep breath that was filled with the scent of him. Even the first time she met him, he'd smelled so good. She wanted to bury her face in his neck and inhale his essence into her body.

She turned slowly, as if pulled by invisible strings, unable to stop despite knowing that she was about to lose what small amount of control she'd mustered. "Me too," she whispered, knowing she was only embroiling herself deeper.

But after she recovered her sister, the chance to have this —whatever this was—would be gone. *Poof!* And she would return to being sad little Azia, alone forever, wondering why she hadn't grabbed at this chance with both hands, regretting her lack of courage.

"What are you drinking?"

"Milk." She felt so unsophisticated, so clearly lost in this sea of interactions between men and women.

"You should try something stronger."

"Does it work?" She stepped toward him, leaving her milk behind. She couldn't see his face clearly where he sat in a puddle of darkness, but his voice sounded like warm fur sliding across her skin.

"Not particularly."

"Do you want to have sex with me?"

"Very much." He stayed perfectly still, his body frozen, his tone carefully blank. "Do you want to have sex with me?"

"I think I do. I'm sure it's a terrible idea."

"We're two consenting adults enjoying each other. There is nothing wrong with that."

She nodded, liking the sound of the justification. Just adults having fun. People did it all the time. Although she had never. "Do you think this attraction is happening because you're the first Delphi I've ever met?"

A strange look crossed his face, but in the darkness, she couldn't tell what it was.

"That could be true," he said, and slammed back another shot of alcohol, then cradled the glass in his hands. "The choice is yours, of course, but we come out of jump"— he checked a nearby vid screen—"in sixty-eight hours. And then we'll be busy negotiating for your sister."

He was right. This was it. Her only chance to have this experience that all other adults had in the normal course of their lives. She'd first noticed her attraction to him in Hell's Gate. He was the first man who'd ever increased her heart rate and made her want to toss out all her good intentions. The first man she'd ever smelled who attracted instead of repulsed.

"Yes," she said, agreeing to everything.

He nodded once and stood.

"Oh. Wait. Did you mean now?" Like right now this

minute? Nerves coursed through her and she laughed awkwardly, at what she wasn't sure. Maybe herself.

"Now," he said, his body frozen in coiled readiness.

"Okay." Fighting the roar of her nerves, she led him to her room, which had a much bigger bunk than his. She figured they'd need the space, since he was enormous. She pressed her palm against the reader and the doors slid open.

He swooped her up into his arms and crossed the small space in two strides. Then his lips were on hers, as he let her body slide down his. She ended up standing on the bed, her lips pressed into his, taller than him with the help of the mattress. The height difference gave her the power to control the kiss. Their lips melded and caressed, his tongue darting out to explore her mouth.

When that wasn't enough for her any longer, she pulled him down on the bed, spilling back ungraciously, bringing him with her so he caught himself above her in a pushup, his lips never leaving hers.

He ate her mouth as if he were starving, as if she were his very lifeline.

Desire spun through her as she knew for the first time in her life the power of being a woman, of being worshipped. She would never forget this moment if she lived to be a hundred. The weight of him, the warmth of his breath as it swirled with hers, the enormity of the need coursing through her. She basked in it.

Suddenly, it wasn't enough. She needed to feel his naked flesh against hers. She dragged at his shirt until his lips left hers long enough for him to shrug out of it. Then he stripped her lower half down to nothing, taking her pants and panties off in one sweep.

"Whoa, now," she said, laughing because it was

wonderful and amazing to have someone want her this badly.

He didn't laugh in return, but stripped her out of her shirt and placed her on the center of the bed. Then he ran his lips and tongue down every inch of her skin, while one hand gently worked her nipple in a whisper touch that tugged and barely twisted, sending bolts of desire through her. Who knew someone so strong could touch her so gently. When his mouth reached the other breast, desire crescendoed within her.

"I want you," she heard herself whisper, feeling foolish, but it was so true.

"I have to taste you first," he growled and licked down her stomach to the core of her. Laving her clit, he built and built a fire that raced along her skin, making her both twist away and beg for more.

Something wonderful grew inside her, a pressure that had her shaking uncontrollably with need. Vaguely, she heard her herself whisper, "Please, please," over and over. She just needed to fall off the cliff, to release the pressure that had reached a screaming intensity inside her.

Her orgasm raced over her as every muscle held tight, as she arched into the sensation, the feeling so good she wanted so badly to have it again the moment it began to fade away.

As she shivered with lingering pleasure, he rose and rubbed his cock through her wetness, the feel of him hitting her swollen clit causing her to moan in pleasure.

He worked his cock into her tight, tight passage, stretching her so much, she wondered if he was too big for her. His journey seemed to halt prematurely when he ran into a barrier. But he thrust past it and hilted.

Pleasure and pain filled her, making her arch back and whisper his name.

∼

LOCKE FELT the snag when his cock passed the barrier which told him he was her first. His brain recorded it, but there wasn't much he could do to readjust his momentum. All his mind wanted was release. That, and to bring her to orgasm once again. But the piece of him that could still think knew it was now even more important to make this good for her. This experience would impact how she felt about every other she had in the future. He wanted her remembering how good his body felt in hers for the rest of her life.

He stroked deep, watching her face as the pleasure climbed across it once more. She was gorgeous. Perfect in every way, her small body fit with his big one like two pieces of a puzzle. "You're so beautiful," he whispered.

Her eyes opened. "You are too." She stroked a hand along the muscles of his bicep.

He gasped a laugh, then pulled one of her legs up above his shoulder to delve even deeper, needing to be as close to her as possible.

"Oh," she whispered, her eyes shutting. "Who knew it could be so very good?" Her question was filled with awe, and he reveled in it.

His orgasm raced toward him, barreling down, refusing to be derailed. Before he lost his mind completely, he pinned her clit beneath a finger, instantly gratified when he felt her whole sex clench as she reached climax.

Then his own release roared through him, the flame that was the core of him lit his hands in a fiery glow. She screamed again in pleasure, twisting under the hand still on her sex, the fire of his flame super-charging her orgasm.

Trying instinctively to complete the ritual, he slammed all his power through her, but it was met by nothing, no answering call of power, no twining of their flames.

He collapsed, his power completely expended in the wasted rush.

Her own flame had not responded in kind. Disappointment rode through him, but he pushed it aside. The sex had been incredible. Surely that meant something. He wouldn't enjoy someone so completely who was not his mate.

Would he?

Maybe they couldn't complete the ritual because she was unable to call a flame. He found he wanted her so much, he wasn't sure he cared. *Mine!* his mind screamed. He pulled her close, her scent filling his head, soothing a piece of him that had been bereft all this time.

It was only as he fell asleep that a terrible thought occurred to him. If he was bonded to one of her sisters, having sex with Azia would be the greatest mistake of his life.

As exhaustion claimed him, he found the thought of any woman other than Azia made his heart protest. In the twilight before sleep, he knew he wanted her and no other.

7

From her bed where she nestled in a warm cocoon, Azia stared at the vid screen, her mind still dazed as the view of jump space passed by in a vague blur. The massive, dangerous felon she'd chosen as her first bedmate still slept in her bed, one large arm slung over her waist, pinning her back to his front.

She had finally had sex, which seemed to be a rite of passage that she'd always thought would be off limits for her. Both Bayle and Dru had already taken their first lovers and their stories of sleeping with men had always brought a pang of wistfulness to Azia. But the few times she'd tried to date, she'd found herself longing to be home, curled up under a blanket, reading a book.

It was this hulking Delphi man who changed her mind and the more she considered it, the more she thought it was because of their shared heritage. His DNA brought the spark of desire, some base chemistry that others didn't possess. That had to be it. While she was energized, a lazy sort of contentment purred through her.

She turned that idea over in her mind for a bit, weighing

the truth, but then was distracted by the feeling of Locke's body where it pressed along hers. It was strangely comforting, like when she and her sisters had huddled together during a storm in her bed, only more intimate, more soothing.

I thought I'd feel different. Changed.

But she didn't. She still felt like Azia, except maybe that her body was relaxed for once and her mind was a jumble of thoughts she could do nothing about. She was tempted to roll over and wake him, maybe see if the amazing sex had been a fluke, but she wasn't sure if that would break some sort of taboo she didn't know about. Maybe it wasn't polite to demand sex from your partner so soon after she'd just had some. Honesty compelled her to admit she would like to have more sex now that she knew how good it could be. Bayle had said it was fun and Dru had said it was over-rated, but Azia found it was neither. It was... she searched for the right word... glorious.

They would come out of jump soon and this opportunity to explore would be over. She rolled to her back to study him. He didn't wake, but his arm adjusted to return her tight against his side, his anti-escape cuff bumping against hers, temporarily lighting up blue, signaling that they were tied together.

He was handsome in sleep. The lines of his face relaxed, making him less harsh and scary and more boyish and classically good looking. Although his nose had been broken and his chest still had shades of blue and green from the damage the prison guards had done to him. She ran a finger over a faded black line, turning green along the edges, tracing a baton strike.

"I was able to heal my ribs," he murmured, his eyes still shut, his body relaxed, although some of the harsh lines of his face had returned as he returned to consciousness.

"They were broken?" She hadn't known he'd been that hurt or she would have offered her med bay.

"Three of them were. In Hell's Gate, I hadn't had enough energy to fix them." He opened his blue-on-blue eyes, and immediately all the intensity rushed back, his presence filling up her small room. "It's been a year or longer since I've been able to heal something so complex."

She wondered if he even knew how much space he commanded. Much more than any normal man she'd ever met. "You've still got some bruising."

"I didn't have enough left to fix that too, but you could help me with that." He rolled to his back, dragging her on top of his chest.

She kept a slight distance by supporting herself with one hand on the bed beside them. She had questions she didn't want him to distract her from asking. "Sex allowed you to heal yourself?" Bayle had said Delphi mated for life but otherwise, her sister had never listed their abilities. Possibly because she hadn't known them. There were only rumors, whispers and supposition.

"It's one way to build power." He gave her a lazy leer, raising and lowering his eyebrows at her. "Interested in helping me straighten my nose? It will make this ugly mug less difficult to look at."

She ran a finger along his cheek. "Oh, I don't know. You look pretty good to me." She dropped a kiss on his nose, feeling uncharacteristically light-hearted.

One side of his mouth kicked up. "Attracted to me, are you?"

"Not at all." She was completely. Who knew she'd find a big, massive slab of muscle so appealing?

"Liar," he said with a grin.

She shrugged one shoulder, conceding the fact. "I didn't know prisoners were my type."

"Not prisoners," he corrected, his voice a growl. "Me."

She laughed and he rolled her under him and kissed her neck, changing the tenor of their conversation completely. Dragging her fingers across his shaven head, she enjoyed his feather light kisses along her skin. "Your hands lit up with your flame last night."

"Mmm," he said, running his tongue along her collarbone.

She shivered, need growing inside her. Without thinking, she softly bit his shoulder, leaving the impression of her teeth there. She found the action of marking him satisfying on the most basic level. Let the next woman who bedded him ask who'd left her mark.

Instead of flinching, he rewarded her with a low hum of appreciation. She reversed their positions so she was on top, and he rolled easily to let her. She bent to lick his collarbone, then scraped her teeth gently across the muscle in his bicep, the one that caught her eye regularly.

She explored the expanse of his chest, feeling the warmth of him between her legs where she straddled his hips, the rise of his cock between them. A piece of her reveled in the fact she turned him on, but otherwise she focused on doing whatever came into her mind. She was entranced by the large width of skin to explore and taste. She splayed her hand across his flat stomach, her fingers almost, but not quite, brushing his large cock.

He hissed in anticipation, and she laughed, enjoying the play between them.

In a tease, she snuggled her sex against his, then pulled back as a nip of pain bit at her.

"Sore?" he asked, as he idly rolled her nipple between two fingers.

"A little, but I would still love to have you again," she said, the thought of missing out from her one and only chance made her bolder than she'd ever even imagined was possible.

"There are other things besides penetration," he said, a wicked grin on his lips.

"Really? Like what?" she asked, intrigued.

"Like this," he said, pulling her down to suck gently on her breast. Then he easily tipped her onto the bed, covering her body with his to work his way down her stomach.

She'd had some time with his mouth on her the night before and she reveled in it. To have someone focus all their energy solely on her was worth the indignity of being splayed out before him.

He reached the apex of her thighs and seemed to get comfortable, placing one hand under her butt to tip her hips to just the right angle before running his tongue in a perfect swipe up under the hood of her clit.

She moaned with appreciation. Her passage might be sore, but her clitoris was greedy. She placed a hand on the back of his head to moor him in place, anchoring him to her as he worked her higher and higher. He added a single strong finger to fill her up, giving her hips something to grind against.

Just when she thought perhaps she couldn't take it any longer, the thought of her returning the favor, of lowering her mouth over his cock, had her cresting into an orgasm that felt almost as good as the ones she'd had the night before.

Her body trembled with the completion and he worked his way up her side, leaving his finger inside her, pressing her clit hard under his palm. The pressure kept the spasms of release rolling.

"There we go," he whispered, nuzzling her neck.

"Very nice," she agreed, her voice breathless.

"There are lots of ways to reach release."

She blinked at him, not quite believing.

He pulled his palm off her sex so he could circle her clit with his thumb to demonstrate.

She moaned and flinched. "I'm so sensitive."

He lightened his fingers, circling, circling.

"I—" she started to protest.

"Shh, let yourself go."

"But you're missing out," she protested, part of her not caring, it felt so good. But even in this, she worried about others.

"The thought of you taking my cock in your mouth is keeping me company while I pleasure you again."

Heat rolled over her with his dirty talk, his insistent thumb picking up speed while he added another finger inside her.

"Tighten yourself around me."

She concentrated on tightening her inner muscles, the act increasing the tension within her.

"Fight me as I draw out. Really squeeze down," he murmured.

She moaned to release some of the need, clenching her muscles around the two fingers as they dragged out and slammed back in, his thumb continuing its escalating dance.

"That's right, sweetheart. Almost there." He bit her shoulder in the same spot where she'd teased him earlier.

The tiny pain tipped her over again, the pleasure pulsing and wringing from her as he held her tight to his chest.

She rested for a few moments, his fingers still deep

inside her, filling her up, stretching her. Then he slid his hand free and she forced her body out of the lax relaxation and kissed him, tasting herself on his lips. He plundered her mouth, his large cock between them. She couldn't wait for more.

~

LOCKE HAD NEVER BEEN SO TURNED on in his life. Sex had been mind-blowing last night, but today, he'd reveled in her pleasure. She'd come so easily for him, and her desire heightened his, making him almost wild for her.

Now, as she kissed him, he had a hard time controlling the thrusting of his hips as his body begged for release.

She smiled a knowing smile as her fingers circled the tip of him. Pre-cum coated the crown in her fist, and he was tempted to reach fulfillment right then and there. But then she was moving, working her way down his body with her lips on his skin and he couldn't wait for her mouth to reach his cock.

Finally, she took his head, covering the tip with her mouth, one hand wrapped tightly around his shaft. It was all he could do not to slam himself deeper. Instead, he lay back and tightened his fists in the covers. He would do anything to come at this point. Working her with first his mouth, then his fingers, swallowing her essence and hearing her cries and moans of completion had been the most intense foreplay of his life. He knew just how much she wanted him and it made him crazy inside.

For a moment, she fumbled, taking too much and then too little. He took pity on them both, and said, "Just take the head in your mouth and use your hand on the shaft."

She pulled back, then slowly swallowed his head.

The sight was the best thing he'd ever seen. He'd never forget it for the rest of his life. Her cherry red lips ringing his sex, her hand gripping his shaft firmly as she pressed down, taking a little more of him in her mouth.

Even though he fought it, his orgasm raced through him, washing over his body like a tidal wave, freeing a roar of pleasure as he came, one hand holding her head in place as his seed pumped into her throat, adding to the bond between them. She met his gaze with her own, a sheen of pure want hazing her eyes.

With the last bit of his strength, he hauled her up to spill across his chest, the feeling of her bare skin pressed against his almost as good as his climax.

8

They'd had two days in bed together, or when they weren't in bed, they were in the galley, which seemed to be Locke's favorite place. Azia supposed all good things had to come to an end. Part of her didn't want it to. She studied the sleeping man beside her, finding him as boyishly handsome as he always was when he slept. When he woke up, the years in Hell's Gate snapped onto his face, but right now, he appeared almost angelic. The thought made her grin since he was anything but.

She stretched, and muscles she'd never felt before groaned as she sat up, intending to reach for her comm on the bedside table to figure out how close they were to the gate. Time had caught up with them. No more midnight snacks or impromptu lessons. She needed to get her game face on and prepare to focus on Bayle. All this time she'd spent with Locke had been an amazing interlude, but that time had come to an end.

A small part of her was saddened that she hadn't found her power. They'd gotten to the point that she could hold his flame, but her own had never manifested. Well, she needed to accept that fact and move on. Normal people didn't have to worry about all this, so why should she? She could lead a life that mattered without a flame. Back in the Interworld, no one would even know she was missing a piece of herself. When was she going to just accept herself as she was and move on?

Today, she decided, sliding her legs over the edge of the bed.

Rock hard arms banded around her midsection, pulling her backwards.

"Oh," she yipped, unable to stop her topple onto him. The cuff on his arm was slightly colder than his skin, reminding her they still wore the bands. She should take them off, but for some reason she didn't understand, she didn't want to. She liked the fact he was attached to her, like that neither of them could escape the other.

"Where are you going?" His voice held the purr she liked so much. He was an amazing lover, focused on her pleasure.

She smiled at him. "We're almost to the jump gate."

He frowned.

"I know, I can't believe the time flew so fast either."

"We should have worked harder on your flame," he said, true regret ringing in his voice.

"If we'd done that, you would have had to keep your hands off me," she said, letting him cuddle her to his chest.

Sadness speared through her. She would miss this, the simple bond of touching him. In just a few days, she'd grown used to his presence and she found she liked sleeping with someone in her bed. Who would have ever guessed? As a person who'd only ever wanted to spend time with her sisters, she found this need to be around him a mystery.

"Azia," he said, holding out his hand and calling his flame.

"Hmm?" she asked as she automatically cupped her hand and slipped it over his, lifting his flame in her palm. While she hadn't been able to call her own power, she'd been able to handle his without even thinking anymore. The color was more carmine than true red, a deep, dark swirl of power. She could stare at its beauty all day.

"We should talk." The seriousness of his voice had her tearing her gaze away from the fire in her palm.

"We've had days to talk," she pointed out with a smile, but a small piece of her worried over the serious tone in his voice.

"There is something I should tell you," he said. "About mating."

Was Locke about to ask her to mate? If he did, would she say yes? In all reality she hardly knew him. Well, she didn't emotionally know him. She certainly knew him in the physical sense. But it seemed too soon to commit to him for life, which was what she would do if she said yes, wasn't it?

"How does mating work?" she asked, realizing she should have asked sooner, but she'd been too caught up in the sex, too mind blown that she'd found someone she wanted to think about anything else at all.

Instead of an explanation, he kissed her, the feel of his lips spinning her away from any questions she had, taking her immediately to the place where all she did was feel instead of think. She could have him again and again and still want him more.

She turned into him, rising up to change the angle of their lips, loving the feel of his tongue as it slipped into her mouth to explore. Below her, his naked body hardened. She slipped a hand along his smooth skin, exploring the hard feel of his muscles and the shiver of need that went through him. A small niggle in her brain pointed out he hadn't answered her question, but really who cared? Not her, not now anyway.

An alarm blared to life, the sound so harsh, it ended her contemplation with an almost physical slap, making her jump and scramble in an automatic response. Her legs tangled in the sheet, tipping her sideways.

"Whoa now, sweetheart," he said, catching her before she tumbled off the bed with one arm scooping her back onto the mattress. "What the hell is that?"

"The alarm I set to warn me when we're twenty minutes away from coming out of jump." All sensual need fled as she shook free from him and rolled to her feet, scrambling to throw on her pants, socks, boots, and shirt as fast as she could find them. As much as she'd enjoyed every wonderful moment they'd had, once they exited the gate, she'd need to be ready for quick movement to avoid a head-on collision with another ship entering at the same time her ship was coming out of jump. It was something no amount of techno-logical advances had been able to fix.

Time had escaped her. How long had she been asleep? The couple of hours must have been more like twelve. No wonder she felt so rested and amazing. Who knew sex was the solution to insomnia?

Locke sat on the edge of the bed, leisurely pulling on his pants. For a moment, she was distracted as he carefully adjusted his still hard erection before closing the fastener.

"Sorry about that," she said without thinking.

"Me too," he said wryly.

"Rain check?" Today, she was bold and powerful. It was easy since she knew without a doubt he wanted her.

He gave her a sweeping head-to-toe look that had her stomach tumbling. "You better believe it."

For a heartbeat, she fought her overwhelming desire to

climb right back into bed with him, to forget every obligation and commitment and responsibility she'd ever had.
She'd throw it all away to have him again. Because a piece of
her knew once they entered negotiations for her sister, her
time to explore this newfound sexual world was over. The
loss of it rose up in her belly, combining with the need to
indulge in irresponsible behavior. Almost.

But old habits died hard and, with a monumental
amount of will, she forced herself out of the room,
dashing toward the cockpit. With effort, she shoved away
the desire, replacing those thoughts with a million questions about how she would retrieve Bayle now that they
had arrived. In a few minutes, they would emerge in
Delphi space and she needed to code her request for
landing.

Surprising her, Locke followed on her heels. She almost
told him to stay out of her cockpit since she couldn't think
straight with him there, before she realized he might need
to talk her ship onto the planet. That was, after all, the
whole reason she'd entered this bargain with him in the first
place.

They both strapped in, and she took the ship out of
autopilot. Passage through the gate was one of the trickiest
parts of flying. She'd need to be ready for anything on the
other side. In theory, there should be no other ships there,
but it wasn't unheard of to come out of jump right into
another vessel. Those were the accidents of legend. She
hadn't come all this way to end up as someone else's
horrible warning.

The ship shuddered as they hit the gate, everything
around them going disoriented and blurry, the XL4003
sliding into the new reality, lights still streaking and
blinking around them to make everything a fuzzy mess.

Then space came sharply, nauseously into focus to show... nothing.

There wasn't another ship in front of them, but Azia's relief was short lived as her comms buzzed with incoming messages that had built up while they were traversing jump space. The urgent ones pinged incessantly as she flipped through a series of buttons to slow the ship into a holding pattern dictated by the automatic Delphi responder by the gate. The last thing she needed was an Interworld incident where she couldn't save her sister because she'd been shot out of space by Delphi's notoriously trigger happy guns.

"What the hell is all that noise?" Locke asked, scanning the control panel as if he were familiar with a ship's bridge, which she supposed he was if he'd been a captain of a smuggler ship.

"Messages," she said, distracted. Before turning her attention to them, she sent her request for landing on Delphi. There would be plenty of time to deal with whatever bad news was on her doorstep while her request worked its way through the Delphi bureaucracy.

Then she silenced the warning bells, sighing a bit at the blessed quiet, and pulled up her inbox on her screen. A quick scan showed both Dru and Caden had sent urgent communications, but it was her mother's message that caught her eye. Unable to help herself, she clicked that first, surprised when a video message loaded instead of text.

Her mother's face, so like her own that Locke hissed beside her, filled the viewfinder.

"Azia, I understand from Dru that you are going to Delphi to negotiate your sister's release. I don't know why Bayle has gone against both my rules and those of the Interworld Council, but she's made her own bed and, for once, will have to lie in it. You can't keep rescuing her from her own stupidity."

A familiar hardness filled her mother's voice. One thing Xandra ElAtal didn't do was idly threaten, so Azia steeled herself for what was coming.

"Since I know that is against your very nature to leave one of your sisters to deal with their own problems, I'm doing you the favor of ordering you, as your superior officer, not to communicate, land or in any way engage with Delphi. If you go against this direct order, you will be in contempt of section 218:23:81 and will be arrested on the charge of failure to follow a direct order from a superior." Her mother paused, true anger in every line of her face. *"You might think being my daughter will lead to leniency, but you would be mistaken."*

The screen went blank, showing only Delphi space around them.

Azia's brain froze, every synapse trained to obey her mother without question. She'd learned when she was a child that her mother's wrath would crush her if she went against such a powerful force. Life as she knew it would be over. Azia stared stupidly at the vid screen where her mother's face had been only moments before.

"I'd heard she was a stone cold bitch," Locke said, his voice emotionless. "But I wasn't expecting it with her own offspring."

Being Xandra ElAtal's child had never afforded Azia an advantage, but her mother's message had left her shaken to her core. It was all she could do not to turn right around and enter the jump gate to return to Interworld space.

Her hand shook as she pressed the message from Dru. It was text for fastest delivery, as if her sister had been trying to beat her mother's message, which based on the order of messages received, she had.

"Mother has found out about Bayle and confronted me. I'm so sorry, Azia. I told her everything. Absolutely everything. I am so,

so sorry. Sorry. Sorry. She is in a TOTAL rage. I don't know why she's so angry, but you need to watch out. I've never seen anything like this."

Not that Dru had seen her mother at her worst. Azia had always protected her sisters when she could, and Xandra had had little interest in them until they were old enough for their powers to manifest.

"Dru is one of your sisters?"

"Yes, the youngest." She'd been so absorbed in her own thoughts, she'd almost forgotten Locke was there, reading her family's private business. But her fate was wrapped up with his now, at least until they completed their bargain. There was something highly speculative in his tone that she would have wondered over if she had any brain left to process it. But right now, she had a massive problem she needed to solve quickly. If she even could find a way out of this mess.

Which, possibly she couldn't. Maybe she really should just turn back around and go home. Part of her, the part that was still a small child, wanted to throw her hands in the air. Give up. Admit defeat. Crawl back into bed and put the covers over her head.

"She told your mother?" he asked.

"It's not her fault," Azia said, responding to the unspoken criticism in his voice, although to be fair she wasn't sure which of her family members he was disgusted with. She had no doubt Locke would die before he'd tell anything he didn't want to reveal, but not everyone could be a complete badass like him. Some people...most people... were only human. "It's impossible not to break under my mother's questioning." Azia had told her mother everything the few times she'd been questioned. It had been years, but just the memories had her instantly forgiving her youngest sister.

"Why doesn't your mother want you going to Delphi?" Locke asked, his voice full of speculation.

She clicked on Caden's message, and read:

Mother is in a high rage. It's apparent that she plans to abandon Bayle on Delphi. Don't let her intimidate you into changing course. Bayle needs you!

"Bayle needs me," Azia repeated softly. Her sister really was screwed if Mother planned to cut ties and let her rot on Delphi. Or worse, be killed. It was Azia or no one. She wouldn't, couldn't, let Bayle down.

Caden had taken a job running the small systems department at the Institute, her ability to fix any computer or hack into it giving her a place where she could do what she did best—hide in plain sight. It wasn't that she was a coward. No, Caden had a backbone even she didn't fully accept. But out of the four sisters, Caden preferred to exist by being forgotten.

Dru existed by being the best at whatever she took on, which was currently becoming a pilot. She'd temporarily gotten a job running diplomats in and out of the Institute, waiting for her shot at another flight school which would raise her status even further. As a speed junky, Dru wanted to fly the dangerous missions only elite pilots were sent on.

It was Azia who lived her life as a stand-in mother to her sisters, who made sure they were okay, made sure they were happy. She worked at the Institute only because she wanted to be close to them, especially when they were younger.

Neither of them could help with Bayle's current predicament. And anyway, Azia was here, now, in the best position to help.

That didn't mean she wasn't afraid. If her mother said

she'd prosecute her, she meant it. She never threatened and then didn't follow through. Azia would end up in prison, her life over, if she did this.

Azia collapsed back in defeat and stared at the ceiling, trying to figure out what to do. If she didn't return immediately, she would have to face her mother's wrath and possibly a court-martial and prison. But leaving Bayle on Delphi without helping her went against every molecule in Azia's body.

For his part, Locke stayed silent, letting her think, which she appreciated.

"Damn," she said, summarizing her plight in one word. She was between a rock and a hard place. She couldn't leave Bayle, but she also couldn't afford to go against her mother's clear order. "I'm trapped. There isn't a good solution to this." She dropped her head into her hands, but even as she fought this, she knew what she was going to do. "I'm going to have to go against my mother's wishes." That meant she would be banned from the Institute and her sisters' lives at the very least. And she'd certainly be thrown out of the Troopers, where she'd made a place for herself, if not end up in jail. Her whole life as she knew it would be over.

"You could land on Delphi and ask for clemency," Locke said, his voice so reasonable, she found her attention swinging to him.

"And what? Stay on Delphi for the rest of my life?"

"Is that such a bad thing?"

"Having no understanding of Delphi's customs, laws, or structure, it would be a shock at the very least. Besides, why would they even let me do that?"

"Unlike other races, we believe a half-Delphi is still a Delphi," he said mildly, his voice calm and soothing as if he feared she was about to have a breakdown. "You could apply

for citizenship and there is no way anyone would risk Interworld relations to take you off the planet. You'd be lost to
them forever." His tone was so mild, she almost missed the
import of the words.

Lost to her mother but also lost to the only people she'd
ever loved. "I wouldn't be able to see my sisters again."

He shrugged one shoulder. "They could apply also. You
could all four live here, find your mates and be happy."

Azia blinked at him for a moment, trying to figure out
why Delphi would accept her motley band of siblings. Then
it hit her that Locke had reached what was to him a logical
conclusion. He'd assumed she was fully related to all her
sisters. "My sisters aren't half Delphi," she said to him,
watching shock fill his gaze. "I'm the only one."

He'd thought there were three more of them. Azia hoped
his plan to get Bayle free didn't rely on Bayle being part
Delphi. If it did, they were in trouble.

9

"But you said they were your siblings." Locke struggled to reorder his past assumptions, trying to restructure his previous understanding. He'd planned to petition the Cadre to release Bayle due to the fact she was part Delphi, although looking back on it, why would they lock her up if they knew she was one of them? He'd been so distracted by Azia he hadn't even realized the huge holes in his plans.

"They are. Half technically, although that has never mattered to us. We are all from my mother's eggs, but we had different fathers."

He'd assumed she and her sisters were all half Delphi, but in reviewing their past conversations, he realized that she'd never actually said that.

A mixture of strange relief and disappointment fell over him. Relief, because by sleeping with Azia without knowing if she was his mate, he'd left himself open to the possibility that one of her sisters was his chosen, a major complication that had been nipping at him since he'd first taken Azia to bed.

Although he'd realized days ago that she was his choice and no other. He'd comforted himself with the knowledge that he couldn't possibly desire anyone more than he desired Azia. The thought of wanting another after he'd had her was beyond his comprehension. But part of him, the Delphi part which was used to rigid rules and structure, was bothered that the ritual wasn't complete. He'd been raised from childhood knowing that his flame would combine with his mate's, turning blue. Now here was Azia, a woman he wanted so completely his hands shook when he touched her, yet she had no flame. He felt like he teetered on the edge of a strange abyss.

Still, it meant all his assumptions about how to handle the Cadre were incorrect. "If she wasn't one of us, why did your sister go to Delphi?"

Azia sighed, the sound full of exasperation. "She's obsessed with finding our fathers. I have no idea why she started with mine. Knowing Bayle, she just randomly picked one of us. Or she started with me for some romantic reason."

"You don't know who your father was?" The implications of not having a true family boggled his Delphi mind, where family was everything. When someone found their mate, they combined houses and made the structure of Delphi's social network stronger. His mother had always said you mated with a family as much as with your mate. Which meant he might be mated to the Butcher's daughter. The thought was so awful, he immediately shied away from the implications.

She shook her head. "No, I've never met him. I don't even know who he is."

It occurred to him that Azia had said her mother's *eggs*. Odd wording when talking about her parent.

"I'm sorry," he said, thinking about the fact that while his family was far from perfect, he knew he could always return to them. In fact, he wasn't sure he knew any Delphian man who would walk away from his own child. He would have to be dead before he left his mate or children unsupported.

A bad idea niggled at the edge of his mind. Her mother was the head of the Institute. Surely she wouldn't do experiments on her own body? The thought was so extreme, it revolted him.

The message ping began to trill, but this time it was a response from Delphi.

"Don't answer that unless you plan to follow their instructions. We're near enough to the gate for them to not blow us out of the sky, but we'll still need to be careful we don't aggravate them into thinking we're the enemy."

She slumped in her seat, the action more forlorn than anything else. "I don't know what to do and the clock is ticking."

"Your choices are clear. Go forward as planned or return to Interworld space." He hated to add to her pressure, but he needed her to go to Delphi for so many reasons. "It pains me to have to remind you, but you made a promise to me."

She touched the band at her wrist. The cuffs hadn't worried him at all, since he knew she wouldn't go out of range in some sort of emotional suicide, and he had no desire to get away from her. Part of him enjoyed that she was locked to him. He may not know for sure if she was his mate, but every particle of his being balked at the idea of separating from her.

If he could just get her to a wise woman, he would know if they were mated, even if Azia couldn't produce her own flame. That would be his first goal when they landed on

Delphi, to go to a temple and complete the ritual. They floated within hours of his home planet. So very close, and yet so far. All his hopes potentially dashed by an evil woman whose nickname was the Butcher.

"I did promise to get you to Delphi," she murmured, one hand rubbing her forehead as she hunched over the console. She looked so alone and sad.

"You did." Unable to help himself, he rested a hand on her shoulder to comfort her, feeling guilty he'd added to her stress. He saw the cuffs and turned his wrist to her. "We can't leave each other and I can't go back to Interworld space." Even if the bracelets weren't shackling them together, he didn't want to leave her. He *couldn't* leave her. But he also couldn't return to Interworld space without being arrested. He had to assume the Troopers knew he'd left Hell's Gate under false pretenses by now. He needed to gently nudge her into following his plans, for both their sakes.

She sighed and closed her eyes. "You're right. You can't have the cuffs on." She turned to a locked cabinet in the corner, pressed her thumb to the reader and the door snapped open. Nothing other than a simple black metal wand lay inside. She picked it up and a beep sounded as she started it.

He realized what she was doing and wanted to protest, wanted to stop her, but within seconds, the cuff on his wrist had snapped open.

The excuse of the cuff to keep them together was gone. Desperate, he knelt before her. "Come to Delphi with me. Don't you want to see your home planet? Smell the air? Meet your people?"

"My people." Her eyes grew huge with longing.

Knowing it was a dirty move, he rose and pulled her out of her chair, setting his lips on hers, both to comfort and to pressure her to go with him. If she left when they were so close, he'd never forgive himself for not trying harder.

At first, she didn't respond, hanging limp in his arms. Then her lips moved on his and he leaned into her, the feeling so right, he knew that even though the ritual hadn't been completed, he would struggle to ever leave her side. What did it matter if she had no flame?

She slid from his arms and sank back into her chair. "I can't think when you do that," she said, and rested her head back, closing her eyes.

The air was filled with the dinging of Delphi's waiting message. Locke had no doubt he could talk them onto the planet if needed. His family had enough connections that he could get Azia on without much fuss. Although, more than four years had passed. He wondered if anything had changed? Surely not anything that significant.

Azia sat for a long moment, so still that he began to worry. Then she took a deep breath and straightened. "You're right. I promised to get you to Delphi."

She was going to leave him then, dump him on the planet before returning to Interworld space where he couldn't chase her. His whole body tightened with tension.

Azia chewed on her lip for a moment before answering her mother's message. He watched over her shoulder as she typed her response:

I'm afraid your message reached me too late. I'll be home soon, and we can talk about why you didn't want me to go to Delphi. I have many questions you must answer for me.

Her finger paused for a moment on the button to send the message.

She might think she could leave him, but she hadn't escaped him yet. Still, she had to actually be on Delphi for his plans to be realized. Once they got there, he would change her mind, he was sure of it.

Send it, he wanted to urge, but he remained silent. She had to choose to come with him of her own volition or their relationship would suffer long term. *If she's even your mate,* a small voice in his head whispered.

How could she not be?

"Wait," he said, guilt suddenly overwhelming him with the thought that he'd bullied her into it. "The Delphi can pick me up from here with a shuttle. You don't have to go planet side." He had to force the words from his mouth. It was such a simple statement: I release you. The last thing he wanted was for her to leave him, but he would hurt her if she went to Delphi against her will and for that, he could never forgive himself.

"This isn't just about you. We're going to rescue Bayle. That was the original plan." Azia hit send.

Locke let out a long quiet breath of relief.

The crisis was averted. For now. But sooner or later, they would have to deal with her mother. Putting off family issues was never a wise thing to do. He wondered what would happen when Xandra ElAtal found out Azia had sprung him from Hell's Gate by invoking her name. After seeing her on the vid, Locke knew a fellow predator when he saw one.

Azia opened the message from Delphi, skimmed it, and in response to the question of the name of her sponsor onto the planet typed *Locke Maynard*. She raised one eyebrow at him in question, her hand hovering above the send command.

He nodded his assent, still working to calm his racing heart. He knew he'd almost lost her, if not for her sister being on the planet.

With a click, their fate was sealed.

Within moments, a quick response came with a landing code, and they were in motion.

Locke watched the blue and white swirls of his home planet come into view as they approached, a warmth spreading over him.

"Delphi," he said, not bothering to keep the happiness from his voice.

"Are you glad to be home?" she asked, some of the tension leaving her shoulders now that her decision had been made.

"I had almost accepted that I'd never return again." He took a deep breath, wanting to tell her the truth. "Hell's Gate had closed in on me. The will to fight was fading. You can only stay sane there for so long before it becomes harder and harder to resist giving up." If it hadn't been for the hope of a mate, a hope that had refused to die no matter how much abuse he'd endured, he would have just ended it.

"I'm glad you kept fighting." Her blue eyes looked haunted in the lights from the control panel.

For a moment, their gazes met and he smiled at her. "I'm glad I did, too." He took a deep breath. "We need to talk about mating."

Her expression carefully closed. "I never agreed to it, so you're free," she said

"That's not exactly how it works," he said, knowing he'd put this conversation off way too long.

"What are you saying? That there is no choice in this?"

Technically, there really wasn't, but he didn't want her feeling trapped, since as an off-worlder, she wouldn't understand. "You can choose not to invoke the ritual, but after it's completed, you would be attached to your mate for the rest of your life."

"What is the ritual?" she asked, almost with a bit of dread in her voice.

"We would combine flames. The red would turn blue if we were mated."

She blinked, taking that in. "I have no flame."

"You don't. But no one else but us would know that." He sat in the co-pilot's chair, leaning into her space. "As far as the Cadre are concerned, we must be mated."

"Why?"

"Because we're going to petition for Bayle to be released into our custody and to do that we need to be a mated pair." That was true as far as it went, but they also had to be mated, or they'd be almost immediately separated. Affairs weren't unheard of, but they were discreet. Unmated pairs didn't live together under any circumstances.

"But if I have no flame, we can't complete the ritual."

"No. But no one else will know that. They'll assume I've brought back my mate, and we'll let them believe that."

She nodded. "But if we did combine our flames, then that's it? We're stuck with each other forever?"

"No one on Delphi thinks of mating as the life sentence you're describing." He took her hand in his, unable to resist touching her. "To find your other half, twine your soul with someone else, is a blessing."

"But you could have a mate somewhere. If you pretend to be attached to me, will that mess everything up for you?"

"Azia, do you think that there is any possibility that I could feel with anyone else what I feel about you?" He felt like he was walking out into the middle of a frozen lake at the cusp of spring, like at any moment he could fall in and drown.

"I don't know. How do you feel about me?"

He leaned over and pressed his lips to hers, feeling his

whole body tighten with need and something else that he couldn't name. "Like I'm not going to let them put you in another room or even another house to sleep in, which is what they'll do if they find out we're not mated."

"I thought you said the Delphi have sex outside of marriage?"

"Yes, but it's a formal society compared to anywhere else I've been since I've left." He shook his head, looking for the right way to describe it. "Delphi was at the same point in time as old Earth's Victorian era when they discovered they had the ore for space travel. The way they think of sex and social conventions can be quite stuffy when compared to the way you've lived your life up until now."

"Old Earth's Victorian era? As in carriages and drinking tea and fussy women's clothing with bustles and formal dancing?" She'd seen a vid on it and while it had been amusing, she certainly had never envisioned herself living like that.

"Exactly." He nodded, seemingly relieved she understood. "Just follow my lead and you'll be fine."

She straightened. "Okay, we're fake mates, then," she said, agreeing without excitement. "Do I need to know anything else before I walk in there?"

"Since you're not from there, they will chalk up anything you do wrong to off-world quirks."

A warning signal rang. Time was up. "Strap in for the landing sequence." She clicked her harness in place, all her focus switching to the control panel.

Home, he thought, buckling in and preparing for the force of landing. For the first time in years, he wondered how his brothers had fared. They would have found their mates by now, would have moved on with their lives. It was possible they had children of their own. How much had he missed while he was gone?

Their parents had died before he'd left, first his mother, then his father, as mates did. He wanted to visit their graves and pay his respects, light a flame in the temple for them. A list of all the places he wanted to show Azia formed in his mind. She would like the planet; he was sure of it.

The culture, however, was very formal and stiff. Now that he'd seen the other planets of the universes, he knew Azia might find it hard to adjust to the way Delphi women were supposed to act. Staying home and raising children was the norm on Delphi. He studied her as she readied the ship for landing. How well would she adapt to their strict rules and values?

He'd cross that bridge when he came to it. For now, joy swelled in his chest at being home.

The landing was uneventful. A robot pulled Azia's ship into a nearby hangar and a computerized voice invited them to disembark.

"Ready?" he asked Azia, who still sat at the console.

She watched the viewscreen with a worried expression as a team of Delphati marched into the landing hanger. "We've got a welcome committee that doesn't look friendly."

"Something must have spooked them. I'll sort it out once we find someone in charge." Although, the soldiers looked serious, in full battle gear, blasters in hand. Unease rippled over him. How much had changed since he'd left? Surely not this much?

Azia stood. "Let's free Bayle so we can get out of here."

Locke frowned, wanting to argue, but held his peace. She'd change her mind once she saw everything Delphi had to offer. He *wanted* the two of them to live out their lives on Delphi. What he *needed* was time to convince her to see things his way. "I seriously doubt we can free your sister quickly. Everything on Delphi requires patience. Whatever your sister's done, we'll need to negotiate our way through it." If, as he suspected, Bayle had snuck onto the planet somehow without a sponsor, he'd simply sponsor her, and the charges would be dropped. He planned to drag his feet a bit so Azia could see what he and the planet had to offer.

For a moment, he was distracted by the thought of what to do with Bayle once they'd freed her, then he comforted himself with the thought she'd go back to the Institute and out of his hair. Unless Azia insisted she be allowed to stay. Well, he'd always been good at thinking on his feet. He'd deal with it when and if the problem arose. He was willing to make a lot of sacrifices to make his mate happy.

"The sooner we leave, the more likely it is that my mother won't involve herself."

"You are safe from your mother here," he reassured her.

"I'm not safe from my mother anywhere," she said, and truth rang in her words.

WHEN THEY WALKED down the ship's ramp and into the hangar, the guards that had surrounded them raised their pulse rifles. A low hum filled the air as the soldiers charged their weapons. As much as Delphi had a reputation of not welcoming strangers, the intensity of this greeting worried her. Locke seemed to think there wasn't cause for concern, but she feared it had something to do with her sister. Gods knew Bayle could drive people to the edge.

She suspected the soldiers were the famed Delphati, known to be vicious fighters. They were dressed in black uniforms with silver at the collars and on their right pec, the markings like every military she'd ever known. Soldiers needed to know their place in a hierarchy from a single glance. Narrow black hats hid their hair, but she would guess it was the same sandy blonde as the man standing beside her.

What surprised her was how much these men looked like less beat up copies of Locke. They had his same high brow and chiseled features, the same blue-on-blue eyes and massive body. The variation between them was so minor, they could have been clones. Unlike Locke, whose nose had been broken more than once, their skin was smooth and unblemished. She found the resemblance uncanny.

When she and Locke reached the bottom of the ramp, he stepped in front of her, blocking her with his body, even as he raised his hands. The men before them seemed to brace themselves for a fight.

"What's going on, Locke?" she whispered.

"I don't know. Stay behind me and let me do the talking. This is some sort of misunderstanding."

She closed her eyes, a bad thought coming over her. "Don't tell me you're a wanted criminal here as well?" It wasn't going to help Bayle if Azia had attached herself to a rogue.

"Of course not," he said, sounding offended.

Relief filled her. Really, the way her luck was going, she wouldn't be surprised if she was fake mated to a man who ended up in prison right after landing.

A tall man strode through the soldiers, extra stripes on his shoulders signaling a higher rank. He wore the same uniform hat, but his had a silver circle in the center. "Locke Maynard?" Nothing in his tone said welcome home.

"That would be me." Locke's stance was outwardly relaxed, but she could feel him coil for action. Although what he could do, she had no idea. They were grossly outnumbered.

The squad leader had not drawn his weapon. "It seems you've sprung from the grave, Mr. Maynard. We were told you'd passed over."

"Obviously, that information was grossly exaggerated." Locke held out a hand to stop Azia from stepping around him, somehow feeling her weight shift.

"We'll need to do an analysis of your blood to confirm your heritage. Please turn over your weapons and come with us."

"Azia," he said, keeping the Delphati's gaze. "Take off your weapons belt and set it on the ground." He raised his arms as if to shield her. As if his body would give cover with so much firepower trained on them.

The surrounding men went on alert, their pulse rifles all rising a fraction as they tensed.

"Step to the side so we can watch her," the Delphati leader ordered.

"I'm afraid I can't do that. You wouldn't want to accidentally shoot someone's mate, would you?" Locke's voice was smooth and unworried. "Azia, lower the belt to the ground."

Moving slowly, so as not to spook anyone, she undid the clip and dropped it several feet away. The tension in the room immediately went down a notch.

"Please follow me," the Delphati said, and turned on one well-polished boot heel to precede them.

They were marched to a beautiful room, filled with gilded chairs around a low glass table. Heavy dark-green brocade curtains framed a window which showed a rolling pastoral scene of vibrant green grass cut short, surrounded by manicured bushes and overly fussy beds of flowers bursting with colors. Everything in the room dripped with wealth, highlighting the riches of the planet.

"We'll need a blood sample," the lead soldier said, motioning to one of the men following them, who brought forward a small black box, so modern it looked out of place in the old world opulence of the room.

Locke put his finger inside and flinched, then removed his hand when a beep sounded.

"We will need a few minutes to process your information. Perhaps you would be so kind as to wait while we finish the analysis?"

Locke nodded and waved Azia into a seat, then chose the one beside her. "Relax, sweetheart. This misunderstanding will be settled soon, I'm sure," he said, picking up her hand and kissing the palm.

The feel of his lips spun something inside her, despite the level of trouble they appeared to be in. She smiled at him and murmured between thinned lips, "What the hell is going on?"

"I don't know, but we should be out of this soon. I guess they really had thought I'd died."

She leaned into him and kissed his cheek, then rolled her mouth close to his ear to whisper, "Why are you treating me like I'm some sort of wilting flower?"

"Because that's how things are done here." His low voice had the honeyed tone she liked so much.

She pulled back, gazed lovingly into his eyes and whispered, "It makes me want to punch you."

He ran the side of his hand down her face, smiling benignly back at her. "I'm sure it does, but until we're out of this gilded cage, let's try to keep your temper."

She narrowed her eyes at him, a prim smile remaining on her face. Whatever the hell was happening here, she didn't like it. The room was gorgeous, but way too opulent and garish for her taste. On the bright side, if this was where they stored their prisoners, at least her sister wouldn't be in someplace like Hell's Gate.

The door opened and an older man walked in, wearing a three piece suit in charcoal gray, with a lighter gray shirt. A circular, golden medallion hung at his breast pocket, the center filled with white gems. His mustache drooped over his lips, his blond hair longer than it would be if he were in the military. She wasn't fooled into thinking he was a civilian. He moved in the buttoned-up way a military man conducted himself. Retired, possibly, since he wasn't in uniform, or so far up the chain, no one dared tell him what to wear.

Locke rose to his feet, bringing her with him. "President Stuart." Locke gave a small, formal bow that surprised her. "It is good to see you, sir."

She did a double take to see if it was really him speaking.

"Locke, my boy," the man said offering his hand to Locke, nodding to Azia at the same time. Politeness warred with curiosity in his eyes, giving him the appearance of a very sharp, nice older gentleman that Azia suspected was deceiving. "I was sorry to hear of your father's passing."

"Thank you, sir," the man who had taken over Locke's body said.

"I understand you've found your mate." President Stuart smiled in a fatherly manner toward Azia. "I am Albert Stuart."

"It was a long quest, but I'm home now." Locke put his hand on Azia's back as if to show her off. "Azia, the president is a friend of my family's."

Azia kept the smile on her face, trying to relax the skin

around her eyes which might reveal how annoyed she was about this whole exchange. She hated feeling as if she were a prize Locke had won at the fair instead of an equal partner.

"Congratulations," Stuart said, obviously meaning it. "Your story will be the stuff of legends for many generations to come."

"I hear they thought I was dead," Locke said.

Stuart smiled a bit sheepishly. "I'm afraid so."

"It is good we got to see you, sir." Locke put his hand on Azia's shoulder. "I believe there has been some sort of misunderstanding with my mate's sister who preceded us onto the planet."

Azia felt a tremendous amount of relief that Locke was addressing the issue right after they reached the planet. The way he'd spoken earlier, she'd worried that there would be red tape and forms to fill out, with waiting periods at every step. Instead, they would get Bayle freed, and she would leave this stuffy, uptight place with its scary soldiers and gilded rooms.

"Oh?" the nice old gentleman said, his gaze sharpening.

"There seems to be some issue with her sponsorship. I would like to sponsor Bayle ElAtal onto the planet, if I may," Locke said, presenting the solution as if he'd planned to do this all along.

Azia straightened, excited that she'd have her sister back so soon. She'd been preparing herself for a long, involved process. Instead, the President of Delphi, a family friend of Locke's, would have her sister returned to them in no time.

A pang hit her when she realized she'd be leaving Locke behind when she returned to the Interworld. He had to stay behind, and she had to go. Which meant no more waking up in his arms, no more banter, no more sex. No more touching his amazing body and being touched. She would go back to how things were before she'd ever met him. The thought chilled her. She realized that she'd changed in the short time since she'd hauled him out of Hell's Gate, and now this new Azia would have to return to old Azia's life. The thought left her bereft.

Albert Stuart's whole demeanor changed, all kindness dropping from his face. "I'm afraid that's impossible. Bayle ElAtal was convicted of espionage just this morning."

The bottom fell out of Azia's stomach. "What?" Her sister had already been convicted, already sentenced? They'd come too late.

"She was caught breaking in to the Delphi record system."

"I have to see her," Azia said, the words bursting forth on a wave of panic. She didn't know what the penalty for espionage was, but it couldn't be good.

Both men turned in surprise, and Azia had a bad feeling that she'd spoken out of turn. But she had to see her sister, had to make sure she was all right.

"That was a fast trial," Locke said, filling the awkward silence.

The president seemed to have an inner debate of some kind, then nodded once and stood. He walked to a nearby painting of a large yellow and gold bird. With a snap, he popped one side open. It moved on hidden hinges, revealing a control panel behind it. He flipped several levers and turned back to them. "That should give us some privacy." He came back to sit down.

"Sir, what's going on here?" Azia could tell Locke was genuinely confused.

"Things have changed since you left. I have lost a significant amount of support with the people."

"But not my family," Locke said, his voice sure.

"Of course not. The Maynards have always had my back, which is why I can speak so frankly with you." He turned to Azia. "Do you know why your sister came to Delphi? She hasn't spoken to anyone about her reasons."

"I think she came to research my heritage, but I'm not sure." Azia had to remember that in this discussion, Stuart could tell if she lied. Not that she planned to fabricate answers, but she'd noticed Locke had carefully never called her his mate directly. He'd allowed everyone to assume and didn't correct them. She had to watch herself.

"Your heritage, yes," Stuart said. "We've been wondering, of course, how you came to have Delphi blood in you."

Azia looked to Locke for guidance. He nodded for her to speak freely. "I'm afraid my father's side was a donor. I have no idea who he might be."

"Interesting."

Before he could ask more questions, Locke added, "Her sister has a different father. She isn't one of us, but I think it was curiosity that brought her here. She is still somewhat young."

Stuart looked away from Azia, his gaze hardening. "Be that as it may, she's been sentenced and there isn't much I can do to help."

"With all due respect, sir, you could give her a full pardon." Locke's voice stayed calm and in control.

"At a significant cost to my current standing at a time when I'm shaky at best."

"I can see you're in a hard place," Locke said, taking Azia's hand in his own.

She opened her mouth to argue more, but Locke squeezed her fingers, silently asking her to not speak. She wanted to plead and scream, but instead, she trusted that he knew what he was doing. There would always be time to beg later.

"I'm in a harder place than you know." Stuart sat back in his seat, staring at Locke appraisingly. "Three days ago, my mate was abducted."

"Sibel was kidnapped?" Locke asked.

"I would appreciate if you'd keep that to yourself. It's imperative that I get her back without anyone knowing she's gone. Roger Fitzmorland has almost collected enough votes in the Cadre to call for a vote of no confidence. Knowing I can't protect my own mate will end up being the end of my career. I would have to step down as president."

Azia would have thought the president would have put his wife above his own ambitions, but obviously politicians even on Delphi cared about power first.

"Who has taken her?"

"My second in command thinks it's a group of mercenaries Fitzmorland has hired. He was able to track Sibel and her captors to the old research base on Aquarii."

Locke's hand holding hers spasmed. "Aquarii? Why the hell would he take her there?" Locke asked, obviously familiar with the place.

"It's off Delphi and therefore out of my sphere of control." Stuart met Locke's gaze. "We both know you're uniquely suited to rescue her. You know the planet and understand how to survive there. If you get her back for me, I'll pardon your mate's sister. That's the best offer I can make in my current circumstances."

Hope filled her. There was a way to save her sister. They would go to this other planet, rescue Stuart's wife, and in return, her sister would be freed.

Locke met Azia's gaze. "Yes," she said, without being asked. She would do anything to get Bayle back. She wasn't without skills to help on this kind of mission. She had trained her whole life for something like this, she'd just never executed in real life.

"It's dangerous. We'll be risking our lives," Locke warned. "Aquarii is a death trap."

"Then we'll risk our lives," she said, sure of that at least.

"You're taking your mate with you?" Stuart asked in obvious confusion.

Locke nodded. "I'll need her to free Sibel. It's a bargain then." He stuck out his hand and Stuart shook it.

"Bayle ElAtal will have to leave immediately, before the pardon is even announced. It wouldn't do for her to be used by Fitzmorland for political purposes."

"Of course," Locke agreed.

"You can leave first thing tomorrow morning." He stood and went to the door. "Tonight, you'll be going to a dance we're throwing in your honor."

Azia wanted to argue, but Locke held her hand tight as he assisted her to her feet. We're looking forward to it."

"You may stay in the guest suites at Brighton Court for the evening, then leave before dawn since you must rescue Sibel before night falls."

Azia knew by the way he said the words that whatever happened at night was bad. She knew her own skills were top-notch, but she wondered if they were up to the unknown task before her.

"I'm afraid you only have until the next Cadre meeting to bring her back here. It's my understanding that Fitzmorland will make an announcement then to discredit me and call for a vote of no confidence. That's in four days."

"Understood," Locke said, nodding at him.

Stuart bowed to Azia, then left.

Azia stared at the closed door and considered how much

more difficult getting Bayle free from this mess had turned out to be. If she had a harder heart, she'd leave her sister in prison to suffer her own consequences. But, of course, she didn't. "I don't want to go to some dance in my honor," she said.

"I'm not excited about the ball either, but we can't land at night, so we're stuck here either way. Are you sure your sister is worth it?" he asked gently.

"Yes," she forced herself to say, because even though she was angry, she loved her sister.

10

L ocke entered the room they'd been assigned at Brighton Court, and did a quick check of the space. Bathroom, sitting room, bedroom, all done in the elaborate style that had been in fashion when he was younger, in the yellows and royal blues his own mother had chosen for every room of the manor house. For a moment, he wished they were going home to the old mansion, so he could see it again. He'd thought of it a lot when he'd first been sentenced to Hell's Gate.

Things must have stagnated since he'd been gone, held back by old forces that remained in power. That was part of Albert Stuart's problem. Presidents weren't elected for life on Delphi, and he'd been surprised that Stuart had kept his power and position for so long. Roger Fitzmorland kidnapping Stuart's wife was a dirty play, but the fact Stuart was struggling to maintain his power base didn't surprise Locke. Normally, a president only stayed in power for one or two election cycles. Stuart had been president since Locke was a teenager.

That being said, Locke wasn't thrilled about going to

Aquarii again. He'd been there before as part of the security detail charged with protecting the first research team sent to study the planet. He'd vowed he would never go back.

Azia stood at the window, looking at another set of formal gardens. "It's so vibrant and green here," she said, but her tone was worried as she met his gaze in the reflection of the window.

He held up one finger as he completed his check, then motioned her over to the tasteful seating area. He'd forgotten how overly dramatic the furnishings on Delphi were, forgotten all the heavy fabrics and gold leaf on every wooden surface. In Hell's Gate, he'd struck all this from his memory out of desperation to survive. Besides, he hadn't longed for what was inside the large mansions. He'd longed for the rolling hills and sunny skies. He'd missed his freedom.

He placed the small, black box he'd liberated when they left Azia's transport on the table before him and turned it on, encompassing them in a circle of silence.

"I see you brought my silencer," she said, arching one eyebrow at him.

"Handy device, for sure. And we need to talk," he said, pulling her with him onto the sofa, which immediately sucked them into the pillows, tipping them close together. That was fine with him. He enjoyed having her body pressed to his.

"You think they're listening?"

"I think we should count on it."

She stared around the ornate space. "It's so hard to believe there is technology with all this old world luxury."

"Don't let all the gold and brocade fool you. The Delphi have more money than they know what to do with, and they use it to hide both the technology and the mining." He took her hand in his and held it, missing her touch even though he'd been by her side casually touching her since they'd landed. "I'm tempted to leave you here while I go to Aquarii. Things are bad there and I'm not sure I can protect you."

She shook her head. "Locke, my mother put me through intensive training to see how to best exploit my psi abilities. When those didn't emerge, I moved over into the Troopers. I'm more than ready for this mission."

"As my mate, I'm supposed to protect you."

A slow grin spread across her lips and he felt a jolt of need spring through him. "You can stand down, then. We're only fake-mated, remember?"

That was true, he reminded himself. He found it hard to remember that since it felt so right to call her his. "Fake or not, I don't want you killed."

"And I don't want to die." She kissed his cheek, just a soft, sweet press of her lips. Her scent wafted over him. "So, tell me what we're going up against. I take it you've been there before."

"I've always known I would join the Delphati when I came into my powers, so I spent my early adulthood taking security jobs to prepare."

"Because you don't have your enhanced powers until you mate and they're called forth," she said, as if she still found the whole concept mind-blowing.

He nodded. "One of the jobs I took was security for a research team exploring Aquarii. The Delphi have a very low population rate. We struggle to have more than one child and a large chunk of the money the government takes in from mining goes to research on ways to expand the population, but even with all that, the birthrate has stayed stubbornly low. We don't need more space to house people like the humans do. There is plenty of room here on Delphi for all the Delphians, but about ten years ago, the need to explore Aquarii gained support in the Cadre. Delphi's wealth of minerals had been depleted and there was a chance they'd find more in the planet next door. Money was allocated to send a team to explore and set up a research lab on the only other habitable planet in this solar system."

"And what was there?"

"At first, we saw only the jungle." He remembered those first nights as being pleasant. "The planet is closer to the sun and therefore hotter. It is very humid. Where we landed and set up base, we cleared a small area and set up camp. Immediately, the researchers began to study the flora and fauna, doing all those things they seem driven to do, while my team patrolled the perimeter and kept watch. Our only run-ins were with jungle creatures."

"Why do I get the feeling this is about to turn ugly?"

He grinned at her. "The jungle and the weird radiation field surrounding the planet made using any sort of radar impossible. Everything tended to rust and corrode quickly, making our superior technology all but useless. Even still, the man in charge of security thought the whole thing was a bit of a boondoggle, that we'd get paid easy money protecting a bunch of silly researchers while they studied a world we didn't even need to know about." He rubbed his chest, remembering an old wound that he'd healed. "But we rapidly knew we'd miscalculated and started adding fences and setting up guns. One of the guys had run into a spider about four days in, so we knew they were poisonous."

"Spiders?" she asked, dread in her voice.

"Yeah. As tall as a person."

"No." She tensed in his arms.

The image of a life-sized spider filled his mind, venom dripping from large fangs, hairy legs quivering. "Yes. The first attack left two of us dead. We'd brought prefabricated buildings with us when we arrived but after that, we moved into a natural cave behind the research buildings that allowed us to defend against them. The passageways were too small for their wide bodies to go more than one abreast. They only came at night, so sleeping became impossible, even though we carved out rooms to make it more livable. We all had bedrooms and even a kitchen by the end, trying to at least give ourselves privacy. The lead researcher stubbornly refused to leave, feeling that what information we gained was too crucial to stop. We won each of the battles, but we quickly became exhausted, ground down, and slow."

"Why do they only come at night?"

"We never figured it out. One of the researchers was convinced their eyesight worked best at night but the tests we ran didn't support that hypothesis. By the time we left, we'd lost four men and the rest of us were injured. Before Hell's Gate, it had been the worst thing I could imagine." He shrugged one shoulder. "Now, I realize it wasn't that bad, but at the time, I wanted off the planet as fast as I could."

"Why hide Stuart's wife there?"

"It's out of his reach and out of his control. He'd have to involve a large amount of people, requisition a transport, build a team to go rescue her. It would be impossible for him to keep that quiet."

"But he's the president. Why can't he just announce that his wife had been kidnapped and simply send a force to get her? I know things are different here, but they can't be *that* different. No one would stand for their leader's family to be treated like this, would they?"

"Losing his mate makes him look weak. He has all the resources of Delphi on his side, and yet somehow his wife was stolen right from under his nose? Not good." Which was an understatement. The mere fact Fitzmorland had risked such an audacious plan spoke volumes about how shaky Stuart's power base was.

A knock sounded on the door. Locke turned off the silencer and slipped it into his pocket, wondering if they sent someone to see why they weren't recording sound from the room.

A young woman stood on the other side of the door, holding three gowns and a bag in her hands. "For your lady, with the president's compliments."

"Convey our thanks to him." Locke took them and shut the door, then went into the bedroom and laid them across the bed.

Azia followed him. "I'm supposed to wear one of these?" she asked, as if she was unable to believe it.

Locke stood beside her wondering what she saw that he didn't. They looked very nice to his untrained eye. But then, he knew nothing about women's fashion. "Delphians are very formal in their dress."

"I can see that. But I will barely be able to move in these." She turned one of the tight, full-length sheaths over to show him the low slit in the side. "There was no way I can run or fight. I'll essentially be shackled inside it." She dumped out the bag to reveal matching shoes. "And the heels are sky-high. It will be like walking on stilts."

Looking at the dresses spread across the bed, he realized that Azia wasn't meant to wear them. She was a soldier, a strong woman of action, someone who had the guts to show up at Hell's Gate to make a deal with the devil. She wasn't a woman who would live her life for moments of dressing up for dances and dinner parties. "We can buy you other clothes when we come back from Aquarii."

"Since I'm returning to the Institute the moment Bayle is

free, I won't need them," she said, distractedly picking up each dress in turn. "One night dressed like this will be enough." She shook her head. "The dresses are basically the same, just in three different jewel tone colors. Red, green or blue."

A sharp pang resonated inside Locke at the thought of her leaving and him staying behind. He didn't want her to go. Mate or not, he realized he wanted to be with her forever.

"You'll have to help me into it," she said, oblivious to his inner turmoil.

"Which one are you going to wear?" he asked, trying not to dwell on the future. He would spend every remaining moment with her living in the now, enjoying the time he had with her. He couldn't make her stay with him.

"The blue one," she decided, holding it up. "At least it has little cap sleeves, instead of tiny straps, providing some coverage." She held it in front of her. While the dress went to the floor, the top was designed to show off a woman's décolletage.

"Go ahead and strip." He tried to look innocent.

She narrowed her eyes at him. "You seem to be enjoying this a little too much, Locke Maynard."

The grin he aimed at her was more like a pirate leer.

Her irritated sigh didn't quite ring true. "These dresses are bordering on ridiculous, but if you're telling me this is what I have to wear, I will." She unbuttoned her shirt with obvious annoyance and shrugged it off.

Locke's whole body filled with instant need.

She met his gaze, slowing down as she unbuckled her belt with precise motions, letting him look. "Like what you see?"

"You have no idea," he said, his voice deepening, his gaze drinking her in like she was a glass of water in the desert.

With a flourish, she slid her belt from the loops and undid the top catch on her pants.

"Now you're just torturing me," he whispered.

She smiled at him and stepped free of her trousers, standing only in her undergarments.

Instead of being a turn off, he found the practical white panties the sexiest thing he'd ever seen. He swept the gowns to the floor and picked her up, easily lifting her, making her squeak with the unexpected move. She wrapped her legs around his waist and lowered her lips to his.

As it always was, the connection between them was fierce and deep, their lips not just touching but melding together. She ran her tongue inside his mouth, making him moan.

He ate at her lips, his need so great, it was like a palpable force surrounding them. His whole body ached for her, as if the last set of hours had been a lifetime. She moaned as he swung her to the wall, and he thrust his rock-hard erection along the crease of her sex, even with clothing separating them.

As if they'd agreed to it, he released his belt and pulled down his pants, his cock springing free. He pulled her hips back in place, her panties now soaked through as he rubbed himself against her clit through the fabric.

She deepened the kiss, her hips joining in the motion, the fact they had the cloth between them heightened his need. Her legs were wrapped around his body, her bare back against the wall.

He ducked his head to capture a nipple in his mouth, sucking on her through the lining of her bra.

"Now," she begged, mindless and needy.

"I thought you'd never ask," he whispered, sweeping her underwear to the side, his cock slamming home, all the way to the top of her passage.

"Yes," she begged, as if she was unable to form any higher thought.

He growled in her ear, his pace furious, hammering home inside her. She dropped a hand from where it held onto his neck to rub her clitoris, the sight of her touching herself driving him to the edge.

With only a couple more thrusts, her whole body tightened as she came. Her orgasm pulled him over, his shout of triumph loud in the formal room as he joined her, his body jerking with pleasure.

For a long moment, they just panted, his body crushed against her as if he struggled to remain upright.

Then he slowly let her slide to the ground, her body releasing his cock, the action wrestling a small shiver from her at the sensation.

"Gods," she said, as he supported himself with one arm beside her.

"You're going to be the death of me, woman," he ground out, pushing himself upright.

She met his gaze. "And yet I could have you again right now."

His eyes narrowed, considering it. Then he kissed her, a whisper soft brush of his lips.

From somewhere deep in the house, a gong sounded.

"The bell for the dance," he said, lifting his lips from hers. "It's starting in five minutes."

Her eyes, which had drifted shut, popped open. "I'll barely have time to get into the dress and brush my hair."

Locke steadied her on her feet, his hands a caress. "We need to be on time, but I could have you again and again, over and over," he said, his voice a promise as he pulled up his own pants, fastening everything back into place.

Then he picked up the discarded dress to help her into it.

"Wait," she said, and stripped off her underwear. "Better to go with none than those."

He kissed her neck. "I will be thinking of your lack of panties all night."

She laughed. "You do that."

He shimmied the gown over her body, then turned her to the full-length mirror on the far wall.

"Oh no," she said, her eyes enormous.

"You look beautiful." Despite the fact they were out of time, he kissed her neck, smelling the cinnamon spice that lingered there, richer now than it had been when they'd met in Hell's Gate. "I am so lucky."

11

I t was worse than she'd anticipated. Her eyes were heavy lidded and filled with spent passion, her lips swollen from their kisses. Her hair was a disaster, snarled and crazy. The dress was beautiful, made of some sort of soft fabric that almost appeared liquid. It skimmed over her body, cinching tight around her waist and flowing over her hips, somehow adding to her curves. The top had little cap sleeves, the neckline dipping too far down into her cleavage, but she knew all three dresses had similar necklines that were far more risqué than her normal comfort zone.

"Wow," Locke said, kneeling at her feet to help her into her shoes.

"That's one way to put it."

"You look amazing," he said, his voice reverent.

"Amazingly like I'm about to have my breasts spring free, you mean?" She fought panic as she wobbled to the bathroom and sat on the small, golden chair in front of the dressing mirror, wondering how she would make her hair do something other than its current after-sex disaster look.

She would be on display tonight, a curiosity at best, with everyone inspecting her, staring at her. She had no doubt most of the women there would have spent hours getting ready, possibly with a hairdresser to help them. What she really wanted to do was find her sister and go home.

But instead, she went through all the drawers in the small table before her, finding first a hairbrush and then pins. Each drawer held a wealth of creams, and makeup, and women's implements, the purpose of most of it a mystery. There wasn't time to figure it out, so she went with simple. Putting her hair back into the bun she wore to work, she figured it was her only option to disguise the mess. Then she dabbed on some lipstick and eyeliner.

Locke had disappeared, but he came back to stand in the doorway, watching her.

"This is the best I can do," she told him, knowing they were already late.

"You look beautiful now and you looked beautiful before." He offered his arm.

She realized he hadn't lied to save her feelings. He truly believed that she was beautiful. The thought triggered a pang of longing in her heart as she used his arm to balance as they walked. She had spent a lot of time learning hand to hand fighting, building her core strength and balance. She needed all of those skills to walk in the blue heels.

He smiled down at her. "We'll brazen this out and be on our way in the early morning."

She stumbled and he caught her, swinging her into his body so they were pressed against each other. His gaze heated with desire as he stared at her lips. "I'm trying to behave so I won't mess up your careful work, but it's hard."

Something inside her relaxed. She'd face all these

people with him at her side. He had her back. She could count on him.

She'd miss this so much when she was gone. Being desired was a heady power she'd never encountered before and she didn't fool herself into thinking she'd ever find it again. Maybe they weren't mated—and without a flame, she'd never know—but her feelings for Locke were so far beyond anything she'd ever had for a man.

Then they rounded the corner, joining a line of people who were announced as they entered the ball.

Immediately, Azia knew she wasn't like any of the other women here. Just as the soldiers at the landing depot had been copies of one another, the women dressed in their jewel-toned dresses were tall and thin, all looking alike in their finery. They all wore feathers or caps in their hair, which was styled in elaborate coifs upon their heads. They walked without wobble on their high heels, beside men who matched them—flawless in their black and white finery.

She met Locke's gaze. "This is going to suck," she said softly.

His lips pulled down in a grimace. "You're right. I forgot how much I don't enjoy these balls."

"Then why are we here?"

"The president has made us guests of honor. We could not refuse."

"That's a shame," she said, meaning it. It was only the force of will that had her moving forward in the line.

And then a man dressed in bright red livery, a microphone on a stalk from his earpiece barely visible, announced them in a booming voice, "Locke Maynard and his mate."

The whole room seemed to pause as everyone turned toward them. Azia plastered on a smile as she moved into the elaborate space, holding Locke's arm so she didn't fall and end up in a heap of skirts.

They moved forward, Locke taking a glass of offered wine and handing it to her, then grabbing one for himself. They stood to one side, as she stared back at the people staring at her, realizing that she'd had no name when she'd been introduced. Here she would not be Azia, she would merely be Locke's mate.

A man strode through the crowd, winding toward them with purpose.

"Locke," he said, shaking hands, then turning to her.

"Morty, this is Azia."

His body matched Locke's—all muscles and strength—but it was his face that had her blinking. While the Delphati soldiers had been similar to Locke, this man could have been his twin. It went beyond the matching looks to the brooding, serious features and the way he held himself. It was only the short length of Locke's hair and his broken nose which made it easy to tell them apart.

He bowed over her hand, but his lips didn't reach her skin. "Welcome to our family, Sister," he said, studying her. "So, you did it then. You found her. I would have bet against you."

Azia had so many questions about the undertones in Morty's voice, but she felt as if she shouldn't ask. In fact, a quick glance around the room showed women and men had separated into gendered groups, talking to each other instead of to the opposite sex.

She wondered how long she had to stay here before she could escape.

～

"I UNDERSTAND you thought I was dead?" Locke said, carefully steering his brother away from questions about Azia being his mate. He had to be very careful not to trap himself in a lie that his brother could hear.

"When you stopped sending word back, we assumed that you'd gone over." There was censure in his tone. His brother was pissed and Locke didn't blame him. Locke's inability to find his mate on Delphi had been a big embarrassment for the family. In Delphian society, it was best to follow the regimented societal norms and not stand out in any way.

"I ran into some trouble and ended up in an Interworld prison."

"That was unfortunate," Morty said.

"Very," Locke agreed. "Where is your mate?" he asked, changing the subject to more neutral topics.

"Home. She's on bed rest since she's pregnant."

"Congratulations," Locke said, feeling a true jolt of happiness for his oldest brother. The Maynard line would continue. "And Arnold?"

"Off on some secret Delphati mission." Morty's gaze narrowed. "What will you do now that you've come home? Will you join the Delphati?"

Locke had always planned on joining, had always thought he'd become one of the elite soldiers when he found his mate. It had been his driving goal, had helped cement his decision to venture off planet to find his mate. Instead, he'd found the woman who could be his, but she hadn't been able to unlock his powers. The Delphati wouldn't take him, even if he'd become an excellent fighter in his own right. The weight of the revelation crashed over him out of nowhere. With everything that had happened, his sole focus had been to get home. He hadn't thought about what life would be like here. The irony that he'd gone all the way across the universes to find his mate, only to have his powers still locked away, hit him like a punch to the gut.

But if he could trade Azia for another woman who would unlock his powers and allow him to join the Delphati, he wouldn't do it. He wanted her. No one else. Standing in the middle of this fussy room, with these fussy people so concerned about what they wore and said and did, it struck him that he wouldn't trade any of it for the woman at his side. She meant everything to him.

He had wanted to take her to a wise woman, to ask for confirmation of what he felt was true. There would be no time for a trip to the temple before they left tomorrow morning. He wouldn't get that reassurance, but did he truly need it?

The answer was no.

He placed his hand on her arm, bringing her closer. "I'm unsure what my plans will be. For now, Azia and I are concentrating on assimilating here and then we'll see what I end up doing."

"I suppose that makes sense. There is plenty of time to join the Delphati after you're situated." Morty stared across the room at where President Stuart stood with a group of men. "I was surprised you were honored with this ball."

"A late addition, I'm sure. Stuart had no time to set this in motion before I landed earlier today."

"True, but still, he's going to give a speech, talking about how you found your mate and conquered the outside world to save her from a fate worse than death."

"What fate?" Azia asked.

Morty jolted at her sudden question. Locke knew he hadn't expected her to speak after their first exchange.

Women were supposed to be seen not heard in society. "You don't need to trouble yourself with details. You'll be safe here, in our family home. My own mate will help you adjust and learn our ways," Morty told her, a wealth of patronization in his tone.

Locke tightened his hand on Azia's arm, which was still threaded through his. "I'm sure Azia will fit in just fine," he said, changing the subject, but her annoyance was evident as she trembled beside him.

She wasn't going to fit in here and it struck him that he no longer fit either. He'd changed, become something else while he'd been gone. He'd become other. What he was going to do about it, he had no clue.

As the miserable evening ground on, he became more convinced. He and Azia weren't going to magically fit in here. They were misfits now. Misfits that belonged together. And no matter what, he'd never leave her side.

12

It took time for the speeches, to accept the well wishes from others, and for the dancing to begin. Rather than participate, Locke slowly guided them across the room, extricating them, smiling and nodding and working toward the door. Once they escaped into the entryway, Azia sighed in relief. He kept their pace slow as they crossed to the long hall that would take them to the guest wing of the mansion.

The moment they disappeared from view of anyone else around them, Locke swung Azia into his arms.

"Locke," she said, a laugh in her voice.

He could tell she, too, was relieved that they were done with their obligation.

"Those heels make you too slow. This will be the last opportunity to have each other, and we'll need at least a small amount of sleep before we leave for Aquarii."

She looped her hands around his neck and snuggled into him. "That was awful."

"Terrible," he agreed, picking up his pace. He wanted to get to their room, shut the door and have her. "Tomorrow is going to be dangerous. Will you stay behind and wait for me?"

"Not a chance," she said, nuzzling his neck in a way he found tremendously erotic.

He'd known she'd say that, but he'd had to ask one last time. "Fine, but you'll need to follow my lead. Aquarii is a dangerous place."

"That I will do," she said, running her tongue along his ear, sending sparks of need through him.

He picked up speed as they entered the corridor, stumbling through the door to their room, then forcing himself to the bedroom when he was tempted to lay her on the carpet right there.

"You're perfect," he said, meaning it, laying her gently on the bed. Moonlight streamed into the room from the window, casting her in a silvery light. "So very beautiful."

Need the likes of which he'd never felt roared over him and he devoured her mouth. Grasping the front of the blue sheath, he ripped the dress straight down the front. It didn't tear to the bottom, so he dropped to one knee and finished the action.

She sighed with pleasure at being free.

Then he scooped her easily into his arms. She wrapped her legs around his waist, and he pressed her heat against his hips, wishing he'd rid himself of his pants so he could feel her completely.

He reluctantly pushed to his feet so he could shed his clothes, then returned to nestle between her thighs. "Fast and hard this time, then I promise to be slow," he said, asking permission.

"Fast and hard," she agreed, but pushed on his shoulder. "But I want to be on top."

He accepted the compromise, rolling so she straddled

him, watching as she reached between them to move his cock to the opening of her channel, which was slick and hot with her need. She worked the head inside her, then drew back, repeating the motion over and over again as she worked all the way down his shaft.

It felt so good, it was all he could do not to ram his way home. It felt as though it had been a year since he'd had her, instead of only hours ago.

"Oh yes," she said, arching back in the moonlight, her body slick with need.

They set the pace hard and fast, him ramming up as she came down. He wanted to meld them together, turning them into one body.

Tension built, the need to come combining with the need to complete the mating bond between them. This was *his woman*, this was the woman he'd waited his whole life to find, this was the woman he'd left his planet and everything he'd ever known to search for.

He grabbed her hands in each of his and dragged her arms above his head, meeting her gaze. She stared back at him, so different from every woman on his planet, but that only made her more special. "I love you," he said, the words torn from him.

"And I love you," she said, the truth of it wafting through his body.

Inside him, the fire that had been building roared to life, a spark morphing into an inferno that combined with his need to form a whirlwind, the feeling like nothing he'd ever experienced. It made him arch backwards, driving his hips up into her.

Pressure built and built, edging them both higher. Higher and higher until their bodies shook. He rolled over, flipping their positions to change the angle and she screamed with the intensity of it, her orgasm jerking through her and into him.

His hands blazed to light as his climax raced through him, the red fire engulfing her skin, and he realized she had her own glow which combined with his.

For a second, they hung suspended in their mutual pleasure and in that moment, their hands turned blue.

"Azia," he whispered.

She turned her head to look at them. "Oh," she said, her voice filled with an awe that matched his own.

The reverberations of her orgasm made her channel clench tight around his cock. He moaned with the echoing pleasure.

He'd known she was his. Known it with every fiber of his being before this, but now it was confirmed. "You're mine," he said ignoring the niggle of doubt which whispered that none of their other problems had been solved.

AZIA'S ORGASM didn't stop, her core clenched and released over and over, as Locke stayed deep inside her. Somewhere far away, where her thinking brain had receded, she knew something had happened to them both, something irreversible and momentous. But in the present, all she could do was moan and grip his hands harder, the blue glow lighting the harsh lines of his face as they were both showered in pleasure.

Finally, he shook with his own climax, collapsing on top of her.

For reasons she didn't understand, she needed to comfort him. She shook free of his strong grip so she could run her fingers through his hair and cradle him close. When her hand left his, the blue glow turned red and the hand she ran along his cheek lit his features with scarlet.

"You came into your power," he said, kissing her palm.

She looked at her hands in wonder, trying to process everything that had happened to her in such a short time.

It was only then that she realized the bed beside their heads had been slashed as if a knife had gouged it. She struggled up on one arm, rolling him off her to study the cut. It was deep, the stuffing from the mattress pulled up beside her in a mass of fluff. "What happened?"

"My power manifested when I lost control," he said, his tone sheepish. "It shouldn't happen again."

"What is your power?" She caught sight of another gash and realized that his other hand had caused the same damage on the other side of her. "The ability to turn your flame into knives?"

"That's about the extent of it."

She met his gaze. "Is this a good or a bad thing?"

His lips spread in a slow, wicked smile that should scare her but didn't. "It's the best thing that's ever happened to me, after finding you."

"But my flame is just a glow," she said, still trying to process all that had happened.

He snuggled her tight against him. His hand traced hers. "Your flame is beautiful," he said.

"It isn't a flame, though is it?" Her whole hand still glowed, although it was fading.

"Beautiful," he said, truth breathing through the words.

"What does this mean for me?" Did she have power? Beyond her hands glowing? If she did, what could she actually do? Glowing hands weren't that amazing.

"Besides the fact we're mated?" he asked, joy in his voice.

She sighed as reality returned to her. "I'm not staying

here, Locke." She wanted to be completely clear. Tonight's ball had driven home to her that she was nothing like other Delphi women. And more importantly, she didn't *want* to be like them.

"I know you aren't." He kissed her, his lips soft and sweet. "Sleep now. We'll worry about the future after we've freed your sister." And with that declaration, he cuddled her close again and promptly fell asleep.

It took her much longer to drift off. Because it appeared her problems had multiplied. It was one thing to know that she wanted him, that she was attracted to him. It was another to know that she'd somehow biologically attached herself to him, while at the same time knowing she didn't want to live on Delphi.

She took stock of how she felt. Different and yet still herself. She hadn't fundamentally changed, or at least she didn't think she had. Besides glowing red hands which slowly faded as she lay beside him, she didn't suddenly have any powers that she was aware of. She concentrated on her hands and found she couldn't even call the power to her. It seemed a passive thing, like being able to tell if someone had lied.

Overall, she felt fantastic, but that could be the mind blowing orgasms she'd had. Multiple orgasms. She hadn't even known it was a possibility. But she would never forget it and her body had been left begging for more. She had to resist the urge to touch herself, her throbbing clit still alive and needy, even though she felt sexually satisfied.

And, now that she thought of it, she also felt content like she never had before, the sense of well-being so deep and satisfying, she never wanted this moment to end. As if she were a new person, one who felt completely sure of herself and had everything she wanted right here in this bed.

Tomorrow they were going to a planet that was dangerous at best. They might die rescuing President Stuart's wife. Worry filled her, but she pushed it away. She wasn't leaving Bayle rotting in a Delphi prison for the rest of her life. No matter how annoyed Azia was that her sister had gotten them into this mess, if Bayle hadn't come to Delphi, Azia would have never met Locke.

She reminded herself that being exhausted would only make things more hazardous in the morning. Eventually, her whirling mind calmed and she was able to drift off to sleep.

13

Aquarii was only a few hours away, the next planet toward the sun in the Delphi system. Locke brooded as they approached, wondering how he had ended up returning to one of the two places in the universes he did not want to go. He looked over at Azia as she studied the planet specs he'd loaded onto the XL4003's computer and knew the answer. He'd do anything for her, go anywhere for her, fight anything she needed him to fight. For her.

He didn't kid himself into thinking there wasn't a fight in store for them. Aquarii was one part jungle, one part muggy heat, and one part nasty surprise. Never mind that Fitzmorland was likely to have trained soldiers there as guards.

"It says here the flora is highly poisonous," she said, concern in her voice.

"That's why we'll have to wear heavy clothing at all times."

"But the data says it averages ninety degrees."

"You begin to see the problem," he said, navigating the XL4003. He'd convinced her to let him pilot the ship. That, at least, had been pleasant. He'd never been able to afford anything that wasn't held together with string and elbow grease when he'd been out in the universes. He wouldn't have been caught by the Troopers if he'd been flying in this baby.

"Ninety percent of the planet has never been explored."

"Because there is nothing there that anyone would ever want. By the time we left, my clothing had begun to rot from the moisture in the air, mold grew on everything, and my men's feet were covered in fungus. And we were the lucky ones since we didn't die there."

They landed with little trouble, the easy part of the mission accomplished. A hot, muggy blast of air hit them as they waited for the ramp to lower. They stepped onto the damp, spongy soil and paused to get their bearings. Even the air was heavy with moisture. Around them the jungle teemed with life. Birds called to one another, amphibians chirped, and something large roared in the far distance. Unlike the manicured rolling hills of Delphi, Aquarii had the feel of unexpected danger ready to ambush them at any second. Or, perhaps, Locke only felt that way because he knew what waited for them beyond the wild beauty.

It had been years since he'd come here, yet the same damp, green smell of plant life that he remembered filled the air. His whole body had gone on alert, everything inside him tuning in to the sounds around them. The roar of the landing craft should have scared anything away for the moment, but he wasn't stupid enough to trust they were safe. He'd buried four good men who'd thought the danger only came at night.

They'd touched down far enough away from the old research camp that he knew Roger Fitzmorland's people wouldn't be aware of their presence. He'd landed them carefully out of sight, knowing his basic, uninspired plan of overwhelming Sibel's guards would only work if they took them truly by surprise.

He and Azia both wore thick protective clothing which was hot as hell in the climate but kept them from accidentally being stuck by poisonous pricker bushes, or brushing skin against plants that caused hard, painful boils to erupt with the smallest touch. Only their faces were exposed, so they could see and breathe without issue. "Step where I step," he warned her as they moved away from the ship. "Watch the plants, especially the ones with beautiful flowers since they're the most poisonous. When it comes to Aquarii, the prettier something is, the more you should avoid it."

She unbuttoned her jacket but left it on as he'd instructed.

"Drink lots of water while we're here. We're going to be sweating in these clothes."

"We only brought one bottle each?" she asked, dutifully taking a swig as they moved.

"Strangely, the water here is fine. We can fill our bottles in any of the streams we'll pass." He started down a vague path. "There are game trails all through the jungle. Hopefully, we can follow them to the old lab compound. But we may have to force our way through the foliage to get there. That will be much more tricky." He touched the wickedly sharp machete at his hip.

It took them an hour to hike to their destination, time ticking by as they marched. They needed to get to the camp, grab Sibel and get back, all before nightfall, before the spiders came out.

He used the journey to consider what his newfound powers meant. Most importantly, he had more options when fighting. The men Fitzmorland had guarding Sibel would be soldiers on par with the Delphati. He needed to prepare for them to be vicious and effective fighters. If he'd had time, he would have practiced using the knives that he now had at his command, but having them was an unexpected bonus, along with his new speed and agility that came from the mate bond. He needed to take out as many of the guards as he could one by one, perhaps while they were patrolling the perimeter.

He'd thought he'd feel euphoric with his powers, but instead he worried how things would play out with Azia's desire to leave Delphi. As much as he wanted to, he couldn't join her in Interworld space. She was faced with censure from her mother, while he was looking at certain imprisonment. Staying on Delphi might be the only thing that saved both of them, even if the world and its conventions would stifle them horribly.

In front of him, a broad leaf with serrated edges rustled. He froze, throwing out one hand to stop Azia behind him. He lowered into a half-crouch, drawing his smaller knife since he couldn't risk the sound of a blaster being heard at the research station, waiting to see what hellish nightmare would reveal itself.

A small brown creature with a smashed face appeared, waddling its round body across the path, three little ones following it, the last hurrying to catch up on stubby, squat legs. They had spines that lay like hair along their backs, protecting the pudgy flesh.

"Aww, too cute," Azia said behind him.

"Don't be so sure. They probably have mouths full of massive teeth or touching those spines will instantly cause you to drop to the ground, seize and foam at the mouth."

"I'm getting the feeling that your time here wasn't pleasant," she said, her tone dry. The lagging baby made a cute little peeping sound as it struggled to keep up.

"When I was here last, people were constantly getting hurt from everything around them." It wasn't Hell's Gate bad, but he'd been relieved when he left. Being constantly alert, never able to relax, trying to sleep during the day because of the attacks that came always at night wore him down until he was so tired, he could drop. After they'd landed on Delphi, he'd slept for a week. Although, he now realized his time here had opened up the possibility that he could leave his home to find his mate. If he hadn't come to Aquarii, he would never have tried to find her. It was only his trip here that had opened his mind to leaving Delphi and experiencing other places.

They continued on, the press of the ticking clock playing in his mind. He would have to haul Sibel back to the ship. He'd met President Stuart's wife many times. She was a soft, silent, beautiful woman who would struggle to make the hour hike back to the ship. He might need to carry her, especially if she was too exhausted or hurt from being held captive to make it on her own.

"Let's fill our water bottles here," he said, stopping at a creek. Azia squatted on the soft, wet bank beside him and leaned over to dip her bottle in the water. He glanced up, seeing a large blood sucking insect hovering above her shoulder. "Stay completely still."

She froze.

He called his flame blade and slashed it in two, smashing the pieces under his boot just to be safe. "We called them zappers. When they bite, it feels like you've been hit with an electrical charge." He twisted his boot back and forth on the ground to make sure it died.

"That doesn't sound good."

"No. Luckily, they're slow and hard to miss. Get stung once and you'll never forget the experience."

Water bottles filled, they continued on, finally leaving the path to drop south toward the lab compound. Midday came, the sun shining above them through the heavy canopy, heating the air further. Steam wafted up from the ground to create a wet, cloying fog. They stopped at the edge of the clearing, Locke was amazed to find that whatever poison the techs had poured around the compound still kept the jungle at bay. He'd half expected the whole compound to have been reclaimed by the foliage.

He carefully crouched behind the fronds of a non-poisonous fern, staring into the camp. Total silence greeted him. No guards patrolled the fences. No one watched from the crow's nest he'd set up that still stood above the clearing. Had Stuart's intel been wrong? Were Fitzmorland's men located somewhere else? But where else on this forsaken planet could they go? There had only been one research trip to this hellscape that he was aware of and setting up a base here was a massive undertaking. If they were only waiting for the next Cadre meeting to announce that Sibel had been taken, then they wouldn't set up a base of their own. They'd use what was at hand.

So why no security?

Then he noticed that the fences had been repaired recently, although a large hole still gaped in the fence across the clearing from where they crouched. The leftover detritus that he and his team had abandoned was covered in rust and the green moss which grew on anything unattended for only a couple days. An old ring of sandbags that surrounded a rail gun still sat erect to the right, the gun itself rusted in place where they'd given up on it after moving into the caves at night, but there were pieces of the fence that were shiny and new in the sunlight.

At the back of the camp, a large, metal door barred the cave entrance. Adding the door had been the biggest step forward for security that Locke had accomplished. When he'd left, it had been relatively new. Now it was battered and rusted, looking worse for wear, buckling open at the top by at least a foot. Deep scoring in the metal showed where the spiders had stabbed it with their razor sharp front two legs, using their own bodies to pry it open. After he'd installed the door, they'd had five days of no attacks, and the team had celebrated finally finding a way to keep them all safe. Then the spiders had figured out a way to pry the door open. His team would fix it the next day, but they always opened it again. Once the spiders got into the tunnel, he set up motion activated guns to deter them.

Two nights straight after he'd installed them, the spiders had turned back at the head of the tunnel. The third night, the spiders had brought enough soldiers to eat through the ammunition. Then they got back into the tunnels. That had been the night that had broken even the hardiest of scientists and security guards.

Locke studied the compound. It was just past midday. Surely Fitzmorland's men would be out and about in the safety of the sunlight. Or would they stay holed up in the caves, even during the day? They needed water. That was one of the things his team had to constantly haul into the caves before night fell. Otherwise, they could have simply stayed inside, safely protected by the blast door.

This wasn't the set up Locke had been anticipating, and it created a problem he wasn't sure how to deal with. He couldn't walk up to the door and knock. He'd planned to take at least one of the guards out when they were alone along the fence. If they never came outside, he'd have to go in. That put the odds of catching someone alone out of his favor.

"Where are they?" Azia whispered.

"I don't know. They should be out here at the very least fixing that door."

"You think they're still alive?"

"I don't know that either."

After a long beat of silence, she asked, "So what are we going to do?"

"Go to them," he said, reluctant to do it. He didn't like it, but he couldn't see any other option.

"Can we get through that door?"

"Probably not. We'll have to go through the bolt hole I installed." He checked the countdown on his watch. "We'd better get moving." He figured there was a large chance Fitzmorland's men didn't know about the back door. It hadn't been on the specs for the original layout and it had never been used during the time of the first expedition. He'd purposely hidden the exit from inside the tunnel so the spiders couldn't see where they'd escaped if his people had to run for it.

Locke motioned for Azia to follow him, and they worked their way around the camp. The bolt hole was tiny, smaller than the smallest of the spiders that had attacked them. A man could just barely make it crawling. He himself had helped dig it, worried that one day they'd be trapped.

For most of his time here, he couldn't believe that the spiders wouldn't attack during the day. One of the lab techs theorized that the spiders' eyes couldn't see in the light. To test that, he and his security team had strung lights all along the ceiling inside the caves, making the tunnels as bright as the summer sky on Delphi, but still the spiders came. After his boss was killed and Locke earned a battlefield promotion, he worried constantly about a daytime attack, keeping everyone in pairs close to the base, going out on only rare excursions to collect specimens and water.

As people died, members of the expedition started putting in their notices, demanding to return home. Finally, the head of the research team had seen the writing on the wall and had given up, allowing them all to leave, shutting down the project. It had been a great relief when they finally went home. It had never once occurred to him that he would ever be back here.

It took some precious time to find the back door. Using the machete, he hacked for a long time to get to it, wondering for a bit if he was even in the right place, before the door appeared.

"This is it," he told Azia, giving the metal portal a sharp tug. The lock pinged, weakened by the constant wetness of the environment. The door opened with only a slight protest.

Then they stood back, looking at the hole. "We'll have to crawl," he said softly, not wanting his voice to carry down the tunnel.

"In that hole?" Azia asked, and there was something in her tone that had him looking at her.

He squeezed her shoulder. "Stay close and pull the door shut behind you. We don't want anything following us down." Locke dove into the tunnel.

AZIA SHIVERED AT THE THOUGHT, trying to calm the piece of her that did not like tight, dark spaces. She took a deep breath and realized that she couldn't stay out here the whole time Locke was gone. First, he might need her, and second, she didn't want to be alone in this jungle, which might be worse than her fear of confined spaces.

With a great effort of will, she joined him in the tunnel. Stale, hot air immediately surrounded her and she wanted to retreat. The wet ground soaked through the heavy clothing, making it even harder to move and she had to force herself to inch forward. Locke needed her help. She couldn't send him into the caves when her sister was the root cause of all this. If something happened to him, it would be like a piece of her soul being ripped from her body.

She pushed forward and caught up with Locke, who moved slower since the tunnel was almost too small for him to squeeze through.

They rounded a corner and an odor so foul hit her, she had to duck her head into her jacket.

"What's that smell?" Azia whispered, unable to stay silent.

"I don't know, but it's getting worse as we move toward the cave."

It smelled like rot and garbage and air that had grown stale and mildewed. It took a long time for her sense of smell to dial it down as she fought her way forward, but eventually, the smell stopped bothering her as much. Locke might have built this tunnel only a few years before he'd left Delphi, but it had deteriorated and there were places where he had to push through small cave-ins and fight his way forward, slowing them down to a soul-crushingly sluggish pace that made her want to scream with anxiety.

She turned another corner and saw a grate barring their way, a dim glow from the large room beyond lighting the way. They slowed, working silently forward into a wider space which just allowed them to lay side by side. Carefully, half expecting to look out and find a blaster waiting for her, she peered into the room.

Four men sat at a table, no Sibel in sight. They were eating a meal, the smell of rot so overpowering now she wondered how they had the will to eat.

She ducked back down.

"This food is all shit," a man said, slamming something onto the table. "Are you telling me Fitzmorland couldn't afford to send better?" His voice told Azia that morale had gotten perilously low. Obviously, Aquarii could send even the hardiest soul into depression. It made sense that they'd be struggling.

"Quit your bellyaching, Harlan," another voice said, this one full of the authority of a leader. "All we have to do is sit here and guard the woman. It's the easiest money we've ever made."

Azia felt a rush of relief. She'd been worried Sibel might have been killed by accident.

"Those things almost got in last night. If we hadn't fought them off, they would have had that door open," Harlan said, real fear in his tone.

"He's right," a younger voice agreed. "They would have gotten in if Nelson hadn't realized they were prying the door open."

"I heard the screech of the metal bending," Nelson said. "Woke me right out of sleep."

"You weren't supposed to be sleeping," the leader said. "You were on guard duty. Maybe they wouldn't have bent the door if you hadn't slacked off."

"Nothing has happened the whole time we've been here. How was I to know they'd suddenly come like that?"

"We'd better fix the door," Harlan said.

"Send Edgar to do it."

Since the men seemed to be in an argument, she risked another look through the grate.

"Not me," said the man with his back to them. "I don't want to be anywhere near those things."

"They only come at night," the man at the head of the table said. His black hair was shot with gray, his features tight with anger. "I'll go help you if you're too scared to go alone."

"We could all go," Edgar said.

The man at the head of the table pointed his knife at the man to his left. "Harlan is going to stay to guard the woman. The rest of us will fix the door."

Locke touched her arm, nodding at her. He could neutralize Harlan. That would be one down, three to go.

It felt like a short lifetime for them to finish their meals, but finally three men went left, while Harlan went to the tunnel on the right. Locke opened the grate and slowly lowered himself to the ground. Azia scrambled out behind him, happy to leave the tunnel behind as he closed the grate behind them. Adrenaline shuddered through her, leaving nausea in its wake.

She'd never been on a real mission before, and this would be the first time she'd actually fought anyone that wasn't for practice. She suddenly had butterflies that she wouldn't be able to do it.

"No blasters," Locke said quietly. "We take out the first guy as quietly as possible, get Sibel and slip out. Easy and quick."

"Right," she agreed, her hand twitching toward her weapon. She wished she could set it to stun and take Harlan out, but the sound might echo.

They were covered in mud, but they moved as quietly as possible. Azia turned at the door to the kitchen area and saw clear footprints coming from the grate. She returned to run her foot across the mud, obliterating the steps, making it impossible to tell that they'd come out through the grate. It could be that they'd simply come into the room and left again. The men would figure it out eventually, but maybe it would buy them time.

They inched down the tunnel, listening. The halls were tight, filled with an awful smell of unwashed bodies, rotten food, and worse. It rivaled Hell's Gate. She tried to breathe through her mouth but the stench still nauseated her. How anyone could eat while smelling it was beyond her comprehension.

As they passed rooms, she peered in to see small, barren cubbies with only beds inside, most still with unmade sheets rotting on top. One or two had a single chair as well, but any personality must have been taken away when they left at the end of the first expedition.

She and Locke got to a fork in the tunnels. To the right came the sound of unintelligible talking. She instinctively crouched down, checking to the left. Just rock walls and silence greeted her. She was in charge of their rear and the last thing she wanted was for one of the other men to return unexpectedly and surprise them.

When she turned back, Locke was halfway down the hall toward two doors at the far end. One stood open on the right. She hurried to catch him. Voices came into range.

"Two more days and we're out of this shit hole," Harlan said.

"It couldn't come soon enough for me. I had no idea this would be so awful here."

Locke turned and nodded to her, holding up three fingers.

Nerves coursed through her.

He dropped a finger.

She wouldn't let him down.

He dropped another finger.

She tried to breathe through the adrenaline.

Then he moved.

"When we get back, I'm going to eat for days," Harlan was saying as they bolted into the room.

Locke moved fast and she followed, rolling through the doorway. It smelled heavily of perfume, the smell mixing with the foul odor, immediately causing Azia's eyes to water. She blinked to find Harlan standing just inside the door of a room that had been upgraded compared to the rest of the rooms they'd seen on the way here. A rug covered the rock floor, the bed filled with pillows, a fan running to stir up the oppressive heat. The woman who sat in the only chair had full makeup on and was dressed in a silken sheath of midnight blue better suited for a dinner party instead of the middle of a jungle. Her hair was swept into a twist, showing off deep blue eyes that flared wide as she saw them in the doorway.

Locke caught Harlan in the middle of his slow turn, hitting him squarely in the jaw. He fell like a stone, his face locked into surprise.

Relief rolled over Azia at the ease of taking out a guard. That step accomplished, they would grab Sibel and race for the bolt hole.

"We've been sent to rescue you by your husband, Lady Stuart," Locke said with a bow.

"What?" Sibel said.

"You're safe now, but we have to move quickly," Locke told her, making hurrying motions with his hands.

Sibel opened her beautiful red lips and let out a blood curdling scream. "Help! Intruders!"

Azia thought that's what she said, but it was hard to tell, the volume was so loud in the quiet space.

"Holy shit," Locke said, stunned into inaction.

Azia dashed the ten feet across the room to smash her palm onto the woman's mouth. "What are you doing? We're here to rescue you."

Sibel's eyes narrowed as she took a noisy breath through her nose and let out another muffled scream.

"She's alerted the guards," Azia said to Locke, stating the obvious.

Locke woke from his uncharacteristic surprise. "Okay then, plan B. We kill them."

Sibel's eyes flared wide with what appeared to be panic.

Pulling a roll of industrial strength tape he'd pilfered from the XL4003, Locke slapped a piece of tape across Sibel's mouth, and restrained her arms behind her within seconds. Then he taped Harlan's hands behind him, leaving him on his belly. "Let's go."

Azia drew her blaster with one hand while she yanked Sibel to her feet with her other. Sibel fought her but she dragged the woman out of the room, trying to follow Locke despite dragging Sibel like an anchor behind her. They made it to the turn in the tunnel, but footsteps slapping on the rock floor heralded incoming guards.

At the far end of the hall, Edgar rounded the corner and skidded to a halt at the sight of them, clearly taken aback by other Delphians on the planet.

"What the hell?" Edgar asked, tripping forward as two others ran into him.

Blaster shots whined down the hall. She and Locke dropped to their knees. She strong-armed Sibel down with them. "Get down or they'll kill you," she warned as she forced the woman onto her butt.

"Stop, you idiot. You hit the First Lady and you're a dead man," the leader's voice said in a sharp command.

"This way," Locke said, helping Azia drag Sibel into the hall that led to the kitchen.

"We're trapped," she said, stating the obvious. There was no way they could drag Sibel down the bolt hole. Not a chance in hell they'd get her out that way, even if they rendered her unconscious. Why was she even fighting them, anyway? It made no sense. She should have been thanking them, crying in relief. Sibel didn't seem to want to be rescued.

To confirm, she took the tape off Sibel's mouth. "Why did you scream? We're trying to rescue you."

Sibel raised herself up from where she had collapsed against the wall. "Leave me here. I don't want to be rescued."

"You want to stay here with these guys who kidnapped you?" she asked, just trying to understand.

"I was not kidnapped. I left my husband."

"You left your mate?" Azia had thought that people would fade without their mates, that they were unable to be alone.

Sibel's mouth thinned.

"If she left him on purpose, they can't be mated," Locke said without turning from looking down the hall. Both hands held blasters.

Sibel's chin came up. "Neither of us had mates available to us in this lifetime, so our marriage was arranged."

"If you want to leave him, why all this elaborate drama? Why not just walk out the door?" Azia was so confused.

Locke threw a disgusted look over his shoulder. "Because they presented themselves as a mated couple. No one without a mate could have been elected president. Take it from me, not having a mate makes you a pariah, not the most powerful person on Delphi."

"But what does this accomplish for you? If Stuart isn't president, you'll still be together."

Sibel drew herself up. "I'll be able to leave him without anyone knowing. We can live apart and not have all of Delphi know what we did."

"So this is just so you can keep your social standing?" Azia asked, so annoyed now that her temper flared.

"No, it's not about social standing at all." A buzz of wrongness filled the air.

"Lie!" Azia slapped the tape back on Sibel's mouth and closed her eyes. They were trapped, unable to get Sibel out without a nasty fight on their hands. She loved her sister so much. But really, enough was enough. They were on a death trap of a planet, three people with guns between them and the exit. Doubly worse, the woman they were sent to rescue didn't want to be rescued. They could kill the guards and drag her out but Azia wasn't a fan in making anyone go back to a marriage they didn't want to be in.

Although really, the trauma this woman inflicted just to save face seemed extreme.

They would just need to go back to Delphi, tell President Stuart they couldn't get his wife because she had left him, then try to negotiate another way.

"So, we came all the way here to rescue someone who doesn't need saving?" Locke asked, his tone saying he was seriously pissed.

Well, that made two of them.

14

Readying his blaster, Locke crouched to take a quick peek around the corner to see if the three guards had come down the hall. Nothing moved.

"We can't drag her down the bolt hole," Azia said, and he was relieved to hear no panic in her voice, just icy anger.

"No," he agreed. She'd fight them all the way and they'd end up stuck in the cave with her screaming until the three guards found the exit and were waiting for them.

"We should tie her up and leave," she said.

"No." Locke shook his head, looking at Sibel who gave him a mutinous stare in return. "She's coming back to face the consequences. We're not handing Fitzmorland the presidency." That was one thing he wouldn't do. President Stuart had been a family friend and Locke had given his word to bring Sibel home. The fact Stuart had lied about having a mate meant his presidency was over and another person would rule, but it would be a fair election. He wouldn't forfeit the office by underhanded means.

"I don't think anyone should be made to go back to a spouse they don't like."

"Azia, we came all the way here to save your sister, and we're going to save your sister. This woman"—he pointed at Sibel—"Is going to go deal with the consequences of the lie they perpetuated." Now he knew why Stuart always called her *Lady Sibel* instead of *my mate,* as most people did.

"I don't want to win at the expense of this woman's freedom," she said, gesturing to Sibel.

Sibel stared at his mate like she was insane.

He hated to admit that he agreed with Stuart's wife on this one. He suspected this was one of the cultural differences they were going to struggle with their whole relationship. He opened his mouth to launch another argument when he felt the air behind him shift.

Instincts honed by his time on this planet, and at Hell's Gate, kept him from getting a knife to his back. He dove sideways, feeling the slice of the blade as it slashed through his thick coat, the knife catching in the fabric and pulling his attacker off balance.

Another man ran around the corner screaming, launching himself at Azia. From the corner of his eye, he saw her sidestep and trip him, sending her attacker tumbling into the wall.

Locke focused on his own fight with the leader, swinging a jab into the man's side as he recovered from being off-balance from his failed attack. He grunted and snapped his head forward, catching Locke in the cheek.

Locke laughed, falling into the mode of fighting he'd perfected in Hell's Gate. He stepped in when most would have fallen back, driving a short uppercut to the man's solar plexus. The rush of expelled air told Locke he'd landed on target, doubling the other man over.

Locke knew the leader would have called his knife if he had the power, which meant he didn't have the ability. Locke hadn't called his own flame blade because he'd been acting on an instinct honed long ago.

Nelson rounded the corner. Locke smashed a vicious punch into the leader's face, sending him reeling back into the other man. They toppled to the floor in a heap.

Locke used the moment to check on Azia, who wielded a knife against the man she fought. He'd pulled his flame blade and slashed at Azia. She fought like poetry in motion, deftly avoiding the lethal sword, her classic style a study in coordinated simplicity. She used her body as well as the blade, her footwork sure and in control.

Time sped up as he swung back to the other men, knowing he had to take his two out to help her. If she even needed help. He comforted himself with the knowledge that she seemed to be holding her own, but he worried that could change at any moment. He needed to dispose of his opponents quickly to be there if she needed him.

Nelson called his own blade as he disentangled himself from his boss.

Locke beckoned him closer. "Don't be shy now. I have a fist right here with your name on it," he said, unable to stop the Hell's Gate shit talk that had been his specialty.

Nelson hesitated, sensing the crazy energy Locke tossed his way.

He feinted right, Nelson falling into the trap with the arrogance of a fighter who had a flame blade. Locke drove his fist into the man's gut, figuring it had worked so well before, it would here. Nelson doubled over with a groan.

Suddenly, Sibel jumped on his back, looping her tied hands around his neck, strangling him. He reeled backward, his airway cut off. Almost immediately, his vision began to fade as he struggled to unwrap her arms from around his neck. He forced his legs to backpedal so he could smash her against the wall. She screeched when he slammed her against the rock.

Nelson and his boss used the moment to shake off his earlier punches. Both men straightened and faced him.

Locke rammed Sibel against the wall again as she clung to him like a limpet.

He was in serious trouble.

AZIA SLASHED EDGAR, catching him this time in the right arm, spinning away before he could retaliate.

"Shit," the man said, hissing with pain. The flame blade disappeared and now he had only his bare hands to fight her.

His left arm hung useless by his side, dripping thick red blood onto the floor. It made the rock slick below their feet as they circled each other. He was badly losing, and she knew he knew it. "Just kill me, you bitch. What are you waiting for?"

He thinks I'm playing with him. But she wasn't. She just couldn't bring herself to take the final step. She'd never killed anyone before, and she didn't want to now. A movement from the corner of her eye had her quickly glancing in Locke's direction. Sibel hung from his back and the two men he'd been fighting were advancing on him. He was desperately outnumbered. They would kill him.

Still, she circled Edgar, knowing when she took this step to take another person's life, she would have to deal with the consequences. Behind her now, she knew Locke—her mate —needed her. He could not die. He would not die.

"Screw this," she said, tired of the internal debate. Reversing the knife, she threw it, hitting Edgar in the forehead with the hilt. She didn't even watch him fall to the floor, already turning to help Locke.

The two men had obviously forgotten all about her, with their backs to her. She moved with speed, her mind blank now as she fought without thought. All those hours in the children's gym with her instructors. Hours practicing hand-to-hand to demonstrate her psi abilities or lack of them as in her case. Everything added up and came to this moment.

She rounded on Nelson, imagining her fist going to a space beyond his body to gain the most power. Then she punched his throat, her hand blazing red like it had when she came into her power. Her fist went through Nelson's neck as if she'd slashed through paper, the crunch of crumpling cartilage and skin and bone filling the air. He grabbed his neck, gasping for air which would never come, taking one step, then toppling to the ground.

The leader pivoted toward her. He had no flame blade but had a hundred pounds and at least a foot of height on her. She'd lost the element of surprise, but he looked in horror at her hands, at their red glow.

"Women don't have flame blades," he said, staring at her as if she were a monster.

Despite his disgust, he continued to advance toward her, dropping into a classic fighting stance, one foot forward, dominant foot back. He bounced a little to get his balance.

She was in so much trouble, since her flame blade required her to get close to him but her gut instinct told her if she did, he would use his size to his advantage. From the look on his face, she knew this man planned to kill her. Fear rose up but she forced it away, gearing up for the fight of her life.

"Down," Locke barked from her left.

She fell without thinking, following the order she knew

was meant for her. Blaster fire filled the hall, the sound loud in the rock enclosure. The big man fell beside her, his vacant, dead eyes meeting hers as his head flopped in her direction.

Locke staggered to one knee, breathing loudly in the sudden silence of the tunnel.

Azia forced herself to her feet. "You okay?" she asked.

She wanted to race to him, to throw herself into his arms. To have a romantic reunion, melding her body to his. But she knew if she touched him she'd melt and this wasn't the time for sentiment. They weren't out of danger by any stretch. They needed to stay focused and right now it was obvious she was the one with the resources to keep them on track.

He nodded, still fighting to catch his breath.

"Can you make it back to the ship?"

"I'll make it." It took him two tries, but he staggered it to his feet.

She didn't help him. If he couldn't walk on his own, she couldn't carry him and they would have to figure out how to survive here until he could. If she had her way, they would run for the ship and get the hell off this planet before night fell, but she said nothing. He knew more about what waited for them in the darkness than she did. He didn't need her pressuring him.

She turned instead to their next problem. Sibel lay crumpled at the base of the wall. Azia could see her chest rise and fall as she took deep breaths, but her eyes were closed. Good, Locke hadn't killed her while getting free. She wouldn't have blamed him if he had, but Sibel wasn't walking out under her own power.

"We're going to have to carry her out." She met his gaze as he rested one hand on the wall, catching his balance.

"Can you do that?" A bruise had started to form around his neck where Sibel had strangled him.

He looked down at the woman and Azia could tell he wanted to leave her.

"I'd rather not leave her behind, if at all possible," she said, switching her stance after Sibel had joined in on fighting for the other side. "We came through a lot to rescue her."

"Not exactly the rescue I was expecting," he said, and she was glad to hear his voice steady and strong.

"No. But if we can take her, we should. She'll die if we leave her since we killed her guards and she's helpless." Although maybe not as helpless as she pretended to be.

"Not as helpless as I'd thought she was," Locke said, echoing her thoughts.

Azia smiled at him grimly. "Women never are."

She searched the floor for her knife, steadfastly ignoring Edgar where he lay dead in a pool of his own blood. She knew when she'd rendered him unconscious and didn't provide him aid, he'd die with the major bleed in his left arm.

She'd made her decision, and she had to live with it, but the need to cry still made her eyes burn and her chest tighten. This wasn't a time for an existential crisis. Now was the time for action. She had the rest of her life to think about what happened here, once she was safe. She'd been protecting herself and her mate against these men. She'd done what she needed to do to survive, but that didn't mean she wouldn't think about what had happened here and wish there had been other options.

Finding her knife, she strode to a nearby room and found a tarp covering the bed. She brought it back and laid it next to Sibel. The midnight blue sheath dress had ripped up her left side in the fight, the beautiful fabric now ruined. She pushed the woman, rolling her limp body until she landed face up on the tarp. Then Azia searched the rooms until she found rope.

Locke helped her tie the ends so they made carrying loops. "This hike is going to be hard," he warned.

She glanced up as she finished the knots on her side. "Harder than staying the night here?"

"Not even close," he said.

"That's what I figured." She stood. "Ready?"

"No, but let's do it anyway."

15

The hike back to the XL4003 was as hellish as he'd anticipated. Locke had done the best he could to heal his damaged throat, but he hadn't been able to fix it completely. The injury made him struggle for breath and kept him weaker than he'd like. Still, he pressed on as darkness closed upon them. They'd landed on a rocky outcrop and they had to climb out of the thick jungle to make it there, carrying Sibel who now seemed to weigh double her original weight. Around them, the light had gone soft with coming darkness.

"The gloaming," Azia said to him as they set down their burden to key in access to the ship.

"What's that?" he asked, watching her punch in the code.

"That moment before night falls." The ramp lowered.

A tingle of awareness shot through him, and he turned, knowing he was being watched. He searched until he saw the pair of yellow eyes in the deep shadows of the jungle. Another pair joined them to their right. "Move, Azia," he growled, grabbing Sibel and throwing her over one shoulder, not caring that his whole body protested the move.

They double-timed it up the ramp and he slapped the button to close the entry as he passed. Azia went to the cockpit while he strapped a still unconscious Sibel into a seat. They moved without speaking, a well-oiled team.

He knew they had a lot still ahead of them, but as they took off from Aquarii, he felt a major sense of relief.

For a long moment, he said nothing, watching the planet as it disappeared below them in a ball of deep, dark green.

"We made it." Azia flopped back in the captain's chair. "We have a couple hours before we're back on Delphi."

"We do," he agreed, swinging his chair to face her. "You came into your power."

She frowned. "The guard said women don't have a flame blade."

He could tell she was upset by this, although why she cared what Fitzmorland's men thought of her, he didn't know. Especially since they were dead. "Technically, you don't have a flame blade."

She nodded, her face concerned. "But I have something."

"Yeah, you do. And it's pretty amazing if you think about it." He'd been trying his hardest to untangle Sibel's limp arms from his neck when he saw her hands glow red. Then he'd seen what she'd done when she hit Nelson's neck. It had been a very hard strike, harder than it should have been. "It was as if your hand turned into a hammer."

She nodded. "But Delphi women aren't supposed to do that."

He framed her face with his hands. "You're one of a kind, Azia. No one is like you but you." He kissed her forehead. "Personally, I think your power is amazing."

"Maybe," she said, worry still dominating her tone.

He needed to distract her. "We should talk about what's going to happen when we get Bayle free." He'd put if off too long, he knew, but they had to reach an agreement. He wasn't leaving her side, but his company created a big problem for her.

"Not now," she said, unstrapping herself. "How bad is your throat?"

"I've partially healed it, but I'm temporarily out of resources. I'll need to refuel before I can do more." They hadn't eaten all day.

She held out one hand. "I have an idea on how to recharge you."

He unbuckled his harness and stood without thought. "I'm listening."

She didn't speak as she led him to her quarters, both of them ignoring Sibel who was now awake, staring accusingly at them behind the tape still on her mouth. With her hands tied and the harness on, she wouldn't be able to free herself from her seat.

He closed the door behind them. "Shower with me," he said, throwing off the heavy coat he still wore and shrugging out of his shirt.

SHE ANSWERED him by tossing off her clothes without a word, watching with interest as Locke peeled his own free. Then they were in the shower, running the processor twice before they felt clean enough to stumble to her bed.

"We can be fast, then eat," she suggested, moving backward and pulling him on top of her, knowing he needed food and hydration to fully heal.

"Okay," he said and rolled free to snuggle between her thighs as she slid her hands up and down his chest. "You are so beautiful." He trailed his thumb along the side of her cheek.

She could hear the truth in his words. She kissed him softly on his chin. "You are too."

"Not hardly," he said, snorting.

"You are to me." She laid back to view his torso. The huge expanse was a masterpiece, the dips and edges of his muscles fascinated her. She ran her tongue along his shoulder as he rubbed his cock in the wetness of her sex that had been building from the moment she'd decided she had to have him. She'd put this longing to reconnect with him aside when she'd needed to on the planet. Digging deep, she'd done what she had to do to make sure they made it off Aquarii. But now, she wanted to touch him and be touched, to revel in the fact they were alive.

"We don't have time for something longer, but I promise you when we get to a place with a bed and no danger, I'll make it up to you."

She met his gaze, staring deep into his blue-on-blue eyes. "Do it."

He rammed home, deep, deep inside her, the feeling of being stretched and filled so luxurious, she arched into it and moaned.

After a lifetime of not being attracted to anyone, she now found she never wanted to leave the bed they shared. She wanted this man, every day, every night, forever. They still had issues between them to resolve, but for now her need conquered everything else.

He set the pace hard and fast. "Feel how deep I am? I'm all the way to the top of your passage." His pleasure was so intense, she could feel it inside herself, winding her higher.

"Yes," she whispered, mindlessly needing to climax. Without effort, she found herself just on the edge, a hair's breadth away from completion. The urge building, right below the surface. She shifted her hips, looking for the secret place inside herself that when he touched brought her higher.

They went on and on, the pressure and pleasure building until she thrashed below him. Finally, the release began to cascade over her. "I'm coming," she warned him.

"Yes," he agreed, as he clasped her hands in his on either side of her head, his breath sawing in and out as he followed her over.

As they came, red glowed, then turned blue as their flames were called to their climax.

Then she crested over the peak, pleasure rocking through her body, making her scream with the joy of it. He crashed down on top of her as his own orgasm shuddered through him in large pulses.

For a moment, they could only breathe, then he rolled to the side, gathering her up in his arms, snuggling her close.

"Did you heal?" she asked, her voice slow and lazy. Exhaustion flooded her.

He nodded, tucking her closer, kissing the back of her neck. "I'm fine, just tired."

With a strong sense of contentment, she let herself drift into sleep.

They woke with a start, an alarm going off. Azia disentangled herself from Locke, racing to find clothing as the warning sounded that they'd arrived back in Delphi space. She hopped on one foot to drag on her pants while Locke dressed, giving her a lazy grin as she caught her balance.

She narrowed her eyes as she dragged on her shirt, then boots, jogging past the disgusting clothing they'd worn on Aquarii still lying on the floor where they'd left them.

Racing by an irate Sibel, still sitting with her mouth taped, Azia made it to the cockpit in time to input the code President Stuart had given them to allow them to bypass the usual wait time to get onto the planet. Locke joined her, strapping in as they prepared to land.

It took twenty minutes, but then they were in the same landing spot they'd been in what felt like a lifetime ago. No Delphati marched in to meet them. Instead, President Stuart strode into the hanger followed by one of his staff members.

Azia rose. "I'm going to free Sibel."

"You sure that's wise?" he asked, but his voice was mild, no censure in his tone.

"We brought her here against her will, but whatever happened between her and her husband isn't ours to judge." She still felt conflicted about bringing Sibel back. This was a small bone she could throw her.

Having made up her mind, she quickly moved to the other room with Locke on her heels and took off the tape across the other woman's mouth. "Your husband is almost here," she said, stopping the woman before she could release the anger Azia saw building in her eyes. "I'm going to release you so you can meet him standing up, unless you force me to leave you tied. I need your word you won't attack us."

Sibel appeared to fight her need to retaliate, opening her mouth and then shutting it, then opening it again. "I won't hurt you."

"Good enough." Azia nodded to Locke, who sliced through the bindings with his flame blade. They both moved two steps away as Sibel unbuckled her harness and stood.

Locke released the ramp, allowing President Stuart and his aide to enter.

"President," Locke said, giving a half-bow.

"I see you upheld your end of the bargain," Stuart said, something in his face giving away the fact he knew his wife had betrayed him. Anger maybe, but it was quickly hidden.

Azia suspected he still had hopes of keeping all of this quiet, still thought he could keep his power.

Stuart nodded to his aide, who turned and left. "How was Aquarii?" he asked jovially, his whole demeanor morphing into a politician meeting with his constituents.

"Dangerous," Locke said.

"I had been surprised when you chose to take your mate with you to such a frightening place." The president's curiosity was plain.

"She can hold her own," Locke assured him.

When their gazes met, Azia could see he was proud of her. It hadn't been a perfect mission, but she had performed well under pressure and hadn't let either of them down.

"I would have thought you'd want to keep her safe," Stuart said, and there was the mildest of censure in his tone.

"My mate isn't like the typical Delphian female. She's a warrior."

Warmth built inside her at Locke's high praise.

Stuart's eyes widened with concern. "How very odd," he said, frowning.

Azia knew that if she stayed on Delphi, she would be expected to remain tucked away at home, raising their child, perhaps managing the household staff. Big events would be dances where she'd spend hours getting ready for a rare night out. There would be no jump space or missions, no waking up to the next adventure.

Stuart turned to see his aide returning with Bayle in tow. "Oh good, the sister is here," he said, sounding relieved that he wouldn't have to think about how strange Azia's behavior had been.

Bayle appeared none the worse for wear except for the worried frown on her face. Her sister was the ultimate glass half-full person, always looking on the bright side, positive in the extreme. But while her blonde hair was pulled back into a bouncy ponytail and her tall, lithe form looked the same weight, her face showed a seriousness Azia hadn't seen from her before.

"My end of the bargain," Stuart said, waving in Bayle's direction. "You will leave with her immediately. I cannot guarantee that she will be safe from being arrested again if she stays here."

"Of course," Locke said.

Bayle walked straight past the president and into Azia's arms. "Oh, Azia, I'm so sorry," she said, hugging her tightly.

"Later," Azia whispered, relieved that they finally had Bayle safe and out of harm's way. It had been a hard, dangerous journey, but if she hadn't undertaken it, she would never have met Locke. She met his gaze over her sister's shoulder. "Thank you," she mouthed, knowing without him, Bayle would have finished her life in a Delphi prison.

He smiled at her, then turned to watch Sibel leave with President Stuart, her back stiff as she limped down the ramp on bare feet next to him in her tattered dress. Stuart swept off his suit coat and placed it around her shoulders. She stiffened but didn't back away, allowing him to cover her. During the whole exchange, they didn't speak.

"You have clearance to leave immediately," the aide said, giving them a pointed look before hustling down the ramp.

"Let's go then," Locke said, hitting the button to retract the ramp.

"Are you sure?" she asked, wanting him to come with them so badly, but she knew this was his home planet and he wanted to stay here.

He met her gaze. "I've never been more sure of anything in my life." No buzz of a lie filled the air.

She nodded, leading her sister to the cockpit so they could strap in and leave this place.

As Delphi receded behind them, Azia was glad she'd gone to her father's planet, but she couldn't live there. It turned out her mother had been right.

She was too human after all.

LOCKE LISTENED to the sisters as they spoke, watching Delphi grow smaller in the vid screen. He already missed the beautiful, carefully manicured gardens, the rolling green hills and the beds filled with blooming flowers. But somewhere along the line, he was no longer the man who could fit into the rigid structure of Delphian society. Hell's Gate had broken him. He was a man who felt more at home in a cave fighting than in a ballroom.

Not that he wouldn't have stayed if Azia had wanted to, but Delphi with its opulent golden trappings no longer held as much appeal. He had mixed feelings about leaving but he wasn't staying if Azia was going.

He did wish he'd had more time to see his brothers and their families, show Azia his family home, visit the temple and speak with the wise woman. Maybe one day, he vowed, they'd come back again, and he could show her all those things.

Azia had turned in her chair, staring at her sister who was strapped into the navigator's seat. Bayle was in the process of trying to explain why she'd gone to Delphi in the first place.

Locke barely listened to the explanation, which seemed to involve a plan to break into the DNA database and find Azia's father. His mate was so beautiful, even in her obvious annoyance with her sister. They looked nothing alike. Bayle was tall and blonde, Azia was short with brown hair, curvy in all the right places. Locke figured he owed Bayle a heartfelt thank you. He would still be in Hell's Gate if she hadn't come here, and he'd have never met his mate.

He still had the large problem of his status with the Interworld and the Troopers. There was no way his escape from Hell's Gate wasn't known by now. He assumed there was a warrant for his arrest and he worried Azia might be wrapped up in his troubles. They would have four days once they passed the gate to put together a plan.

Once they exited from jump space, they would be vulnerable. If somehow the Troopers found out they were coming, they could simply station someone on one side of the gate and arrest them when they emerged from the other side.

He and Azia had one thing going in their favor. The Troopers wouldn't expect him to leave Delphi. After all, why would any sane person leave safety? That's if they even knew he was on Delphi to begin with. Which he figured they didn't. Unless Xandra ElAtal told them.

He shut his eyes, shoving aside his unease at the thought of Azia's mother. They just needed to get into jump and he'd come up with a plan.

"Buckle in. Coordinates set, jump in five minutes." Azia checked the numbers one last time, then sat back, waiting for this last tricky moment when there was the remote chance a ship would come out of jump just as they were entering.

Bayle slid into her seat behind Azia again without a word. They were far from done with their conversation, but Azia had a gut feeling she was never going to make sense of Bayle's choices. She would never be impulsive to the point of being rash, and she couldn't understand someone who acted before they thought, the way her sister did. Locke sat silent beside her, seemingly lost in thought.

Azia's gut twisted with the uncertainty still between them. Once they entered jump, she and Locke could have a much-needed conversation about the future. She supposed they could go to the Dantham Quadrant. There were several planets there that could be options, one of which was supposed to be a bright spot in an otherwise lawless set of outposts. With their powers, they were a formidable team when it came to hand-to-hand fighting.

"Prepare to jump in one minute," the ship announced.

"We've done it," Bayle breathed. "All that worry for nothing, as usual." She turned to smile at Azia. "I always tell you things work out and they do."

Azia let out a sigh, the exhale still going as the warning sensors went crazy. For a split second, Azia thought she had engine troubles. Then a star cruiser exited the gate, the massive ship materializing from jump, heading straight at them.

"Ship!" Bayle screamed, grabbing onto her harness so wildly that Azia could see her flailing in her side vision.

Azia jerked the XL4003 into a ninety-degree dive, forcing the thruster bar all the way to the console. She had to resist the urge to throw on brakes, which would take her maneuverability to zero.

"Come on," she begged, throwing her weight onto the hand-sized bar despite the fact there was nowhere else for it to go.

The warning siren screamed louder, and the vid screen filled with the massive white craft, the circular communications dishes poised at the edge of the bow suddenly sparked, snapping free as part of Azia's ship scraped them away from their moorings.

Helpless, Azia watched in horror as her ship stuttered past the star cruiser, catching an occasional piece of the ship, but the XL4003's shields held.

"Just a little more and we'll be past," she whispered, unable to do anything else she wasn't already doing in this moment.

The sensors flashed a red warning as the shields burned through their lifespan.

The two ships skimmed past each other, the rear

shielding on the XL4003 taking a hit that made everything in the cockpit shudder. The ship's warning system reported out the damage in an endless scroll. Azia slapped off the incessant buzzing, unable to think past the noise.

Then just as suddenly as it happened, they were free, drifting, staring at Delphi space, the cruiser behind them. Azia sat blinking, her heart still galloping. She tried to calm her breath as it sawed in and out. How they'd made it, she wasn't sure. The pilot of the cruiser must have adjusted in the opposite direction.

Azia kicked off diagnostics on the shields, finding them down to ten percent. They'd almost died, right here at the jump gate.

Locke reached for her hand and they both sat there for a long moment. "I love you," he said, meeting her gaze.

"I love you." And she did, with all her heart. Their time together had almost been cut short.

"We're staying together. No matter what. I choose you, because of you. Not because of fate. I loved you before you could call your flame. You are my chosen."

She nodded, having just seen their lives flash in front of her eyes. "I choose you," she said.

Locke made her feel safe. He may have his moments of being too overbearing, but after seeing how he was raised, seeing how he must have always thought of women as ornamental flowers to be protected, she knew he tried very hard to let her be herself. He worked with her as a team when things went south, and they had each other's backs. He was worth a life on the outer rims.

"This is really uncomfortable and mushy," Bayle said from behind them.

Azia swung around to face her. "You know what was

really uncomfortable? Getting you out of a life sentence by risking our lives."

Bayle's mouth snapped shut.

A loud clang rang through the ship, a shudder shaking their chairs.

"What the hell was that?"

"I'm not sure," Locke said, searching the damage logs on the co-pilot's screen before him.

Azia tried to accelerate, but while the ship's engines whined, they only limped forward a few feet and stopped, hanging in space despite the thrusters attempting to do their job.

It was almost as if... she flipped through her screens showing the outside of the ship. "There," she said, zooming in with a camera to the giant attachment that was secured to the rear of the ship.

They were caught like a fish on a hook.

Knowing it was futile to resist, she cut the engines.

"Why did you cut power?" Bayle asked, panic lacing her tone.

Azia sat back in her captain's chair, a growing sense of doom filling her. "We aren't getting free."

The star cruiser reeled them in slowly but surely, grinding them closer.

"Who?" Bayle asked.

"Your mother," Locke guessed.

"Yeah," Azia agreed.

Her mother. She'd put off developing a plan to deal with her mother, despite knowing the confrontation was coming. She'd let it slip from her mind because she didn't want to think about something else that would be hard. She wished now she'd come up with a strategy while she'd had a chance.

Yet another ding announced an incoming video from their captor.

"Whatever you do, don't answer," Bayle said, panic in her voice.

"Not answering only puts off the inevitable." Azia hit accept, dread writhing inside her.

"Oh, shit," Bayle whispered as they stared at the image of their mother standing on the bridge of the other ship.

"I see you've found your sister," Xandra ElAtal said, looking as she always did, perfectly turned out in her black Trooper's uniform, her high-heeled black boots adding to her short stature. Her beautiful features were overridden by the deep frown on her face, making her appear as frightening as ever. Her dark brown hair was up in a severe twist, hidden under the tall, brimmed hat with its silver falcon spreading its wings to show she was an officer of high rank.

In the past, Azia would hang her head and take what was coming, trying to placate her mother. She would take whatever came her way meekly.

Now, she'd realized she just wasn't that person any longer.

"Yes, I found Bayle," Azia said, knowing she was in for a world of trouble. She'd disobeyed a direct order. That kind of disobedience wasn't tolerated.

"I expressly told you not to go to Delphi." Her mother's voice was calm and rational and furious.

"You did." There was no use prevaricating or arguing.

"You did not follow a direct order *from me*." The small lift of her mother's brows telegraphed her displeasure, as if she still found it hard to believe.

"That's correct." The time had come where Azia had to deal with the issue of her mother. Azia knew she had to move on from blindly following her mother's dictates. She wasn't the scared little girl alone in the nursery when her friend Riley was ripped away from her. She was a grown woman, in charge of her own destiny.

"I will see you on my ship in twenty minutes to hear your explanation." Xandra turned her attention to Bayle. "And you will tell me why you went to Delphi in the first place. I'm sending a team to escort you both." Their mother glared at them in anger for another long moment before leaning forward to smash her finger on the disconnect button.

The screen went blank.

"Oh, shit," Bayle said again.

"Yeah." Azia slumped back in the chair, feeling as if she were ten years old and caught stealing cookies from the mess hall. When was she ever going to leave her fear behind? What could this woman really do to her? Besides put her in jail, have her thrown out of the Troopers or toss her out to live on the streets? Or possibly do to her whatever she'd done to Riley.

She might kill me.

She forced herself to think the words. But would her mother really do that? Azia was an adult now, not some child with no rights. Although, after seeing Hell's Gate, prison could be worse than death.

Beside her, Locke sat silent, his presence next to her steadying.

"She's really angry," Bayle said, stating the obvious.

"Yes." She needed to either finally step up or accept her status in life as always being under her mother's thumb. Living in this limbo wasn't feasible any longer. She had a mate and a life for them to live together.

Bayle pulled her legs up to her chest, curling into a

sitting ball. "She ordered you not to rescue me from Delphi?"

"She did."

"Well, that wasn't very motherly of her."

Azia opened her mouth to try to soften the blow but then closed it when she found she had nothing to say. Bayle always saw things in a positive light, always wanted to look on the bright side. But they had both done something they knew their mother wouldn't like and now they would have to pay the piper.

Azia watched as her ship was slowly reeled closer to the star cruiser, bringing her toward her destiny at the speed of a crawl. She wanted to run. Hide. But those weren't options. And, really, she'd known the day would come when she'd have to deal with this. She couldn't spend her whole adult life following her mother's dictates, trying to make up for something she'd never been able to control in the first place.

There had been no way she could have guessed that it was only through finding her mate that she would access her own powers.

An idea niggled at the back of her mind. Her mother wanted Azia to have psi powers and to be able to study those powers more than she wanted anything else. It was knowledge that her mother craved, knowledge she would commit unspeakable acts for, and here Azia sat, with something her mother wanted above all else.

She stared down at her hand and concentrated, relieved to see it turn red when she called it.

She looked at Locke, letting the red fade. "I have an idea that might get us out of this."

"Tell me what I can do to support you," he said simply.

She leaned over and kissed him. "I'm going to bargain with her. Trade her studying my powers for our freedom."

"Okay," he said, and she could feel the truth of his trust in her.

"I may have to let her study you as well," she acknowledged, knowing once she revealed her powers she'd have to mention his. Her mother would want them as a set.

Locke paused for a moment, then said, "I go where you go."

She flashed him a smile, then turned to her sister. "Do you want me to try to bargain for you as well? You can come with us when we leave." If this works, she added silently. Because maybe it wouldn't.

"Where?"

"I don't know yet, but probably the outer rims." She caught Locke's gaze, and he nodded.

Bayle sat totally still for a moment. "She won't let us all go. She has to have someone to punish or she won't feel like she's won."

"You don't know that."

"Azia." She shook her head sorrowfully. "I do. She always has to feel like she wins. It's part of who she is. I'll stay, for a while at least, and give you time to escape her."

"That's not a good idea." Worry at Bayle's fate made Azia's anxiety rise.

Bayle leaned toward her. "Please let me do this for you. If you don't, I'll feel horrible for the rest of my life. I'm the reason we're in this mess to begin with. I have to make it up to you."

"If you're sure?"

"I am," Bayle said, without any excitement in her voice, just worried dread.

For the first time, Azia realized her sister had grown up somewhere along the way. Bayle was a woman now, twenty-five years old. If she didn't want to be saved, Azia couldn't save her.

"Okay," she agreed, pushing aside her worries.

With a deep breath, Azia climbed to her feet, finally facing her biggest fear... her mother.

A loud bang signaled a docking port had attached to the XL4003's side, then a polite knock sounded on the aft door. The three of them looked at each other. Locke rose to answer, a piece of his hindbrain geared up to fight, but he calmed himself.

Xandra ElAtal wasn't going to kill his mate. She might hurt Azia, but it would be mental not physical harm. While he did not want anyone hurting Azia in any way, he was smart enough to know not to stand between his mate and her mother. Sometimes, you had to let people fight their own battles, and, as much as it pained him, this was one of those times.

A young man wearing the stripes of a Trooper Lieutenant entered the bridge and bowed. "If you'd be so kind as to follow me, I'll take you both to your mother."

The women stood and Locke fell in beside Azia, taking her hand and giving it a squeeze to reassure her that they would get through this together. One way or another. If she couldn't negotiate them out of this, then he would step in with other options. He wasn't above killing to protect her if he had to, although no matter what happened, he wasn't killing Azia's mother. No matter how much she might deserve it.

Worry pinched Azia's face but she nodded at him. She wasn't panicking or breaking down. As always, his mate could be relied upon in a crisis.

Locke assumed they'd go to the bridge, but instead they were taken to a laboratory, the room much larger than he'd anticipated, complete with long lab tables and shelving units with delicate equipment stored behind heavy duty plas covers to keep them from sliding around as the ship moved. In a place where space was a premium, a large section of the cruiser had been devoted to this room. That meant this ship was Xandra's personal vessel, decked out so even on a simple transport, she could conduct her experiments. The extraordinary indulgence of it signaled just how much standing she had within the Troopers.

Xandra stood beside a piece of lab equipment, wearing a white coat over her uniform, writing in a paper notebook. She ignored them despite the fact she had to know they were there. He was struck by how short she was, despite wearing tall black boots. How could such a small package create so much fear?

Neither Azia or Bayle spoke, although Bayle put her hands on her hips and sighed loudly. Azia shot her a cautionary grimace at her and shook her head, obviously warning her sister not to do something stupid.

Locke found the whole theatrical aspect perplexing. Why call them here only to make them wait? Why make them stand before her as if they were children? But since this wasn't his family, he kept his mouth shut and leaned against the wall.

Minutes stretched.

He found himself idly studying Azia's mother, cataloguing the few things she and Azia had physically in common. Like their general shape and the color of their hair. But where Azia was all soft lines, her mother had sharp edges.

Xandra held a lot of the cards in this situation. She could put him back into Hell's Gate. And she might. This woman, who let her daughters stand at attention before her for no other reason than that she could, wouldn't care that separating he and Azia would cause them irreparable harm, and most likely lead to their deaths. Which meant that he needed to spend this time crafting a backup plan.

He silently faded back into the doorway and studied the comings and goings of the people in the hallway. No one met his gaze, no one questioned what he was doing. They all kept their heads down and went about their business.

Surveying the crew who passed him, he could tell they had only a few warriors. Based on the white lab coats, it appeared to be a group of mostly scientists, going about their work. Xandra had hauled a whole group of people with her simply because she had to go to Delphi to deal with this situation. He was positive these people had nothing to do with Bayle and Azia, and everything to do with Xandra's own hubris.

Why hadn't she left the cannon fodder at home to do their experiments there? Why bring them with her? As he stood there, he counted five people who were meant to fight, easily spotted since they were the only ones dressed in uniform. They must be her security team. He doubled it to ten for good measure. A lot to handle, but not an army. Plus, he'd have Azia on his side in this fight.

He stepped back into the lab to find everyone still in their places. He debated if he'd need to take Azia's mother hostage to free them. He began turning the idea over in his mind, carefully placing the pieces together of a bold and, most likely, foolhardy plan. But better to die in an attempt of freedom than be separated from Azia.

"You two have caused a major incident with your irresponsible behavior." Xandra put down her pen and finally focused on her daughters. "I would like an explanation."

Azia stepped forward, partially blocking her sister. "Bayle reached out to me to let me know she'd been put in a Delphi jail—"

"Stop." Xandra raised a hand. "Bayle, you begin. Start from when you stole my notebook."

Bayle straightened her shoulders, brushing her blonde hair back from her face. "I've always wondered who my father was, so I took your notebook to read your notes on how you ran the experiment."

Xandra raised a hand again. "You've been forbidden from entering my labs or office without an escort, yet you did it anyway."

Bayle nodded but said nothing to defend herself. She didn't look the least bit repentant. Locke hadn't really considered how different the sisters were in their personalities, but they were almost night and day.

Her mother narrowed her eyes. "Why?"

Bayle gave a half-hearted shrug. "I...I couldn't help myself."

Locke found it interesting she told her mother the truth. Leading him to wonder why she couldn't help stealing things.

Xandra slapped her hand on the table, making everyone jump. "If you know where you came from it ruins the results of the experiment. I've explained that to you at least a dozen times."

"You don't know that," Bayle countered. "Besides, I can't find any information on my father's people. No one has ever written anything about the Warfran as far as I can tell."

Xandra drummed her fingers on the lab table, her eyes narrowing. "But you didn't go to the place which spawned half your DNA. You went to Delphi. Why is that?"

Locke realized she was still gathering data on the experiment. This wasn't a mother worried or upset for a child, wanting to shield them from a bad experience or keep them from doing something foolish. Xandra had some frustration mixed in, but mainly she projected cold observation.

"When I couldn't find information on my own people, I went to find Azia's father for her instead. She deserves to have something good come out of this. You have never been kind to her." Bayle shrugged. "Besides, I just started with the first one of us."

Xandra stared at her second daughter for a long, uncomfortable moment, then shook her head. "This is the last time you steal from anyone, power or no power, unless I specifically send you on a mission. Steal even a spoon from the mess hall, or a rock from the atrium, and I'll have you sent to the deep lab, where your contribution to the Institute will be of a more basic nature. You take even the smallest item, and that will be it for you."

"Mother," Azia said.

Xandra ignored her. "You've had all the warnings you're going to have from me, Bayle. From now on, you will no longer be allowed to leave the grounds of the Institute. If you do, I'll have you hunted down and confined to the sub-basement. And if you think I'll change my mind, you're sorely mistaken."

"I'll be under this restriction for how long?" Bayle asked.

"For the rest of your life. You're obviously not trustworthy to be out on your own." A promise threaded through Xandra's words. This wasn't a threat, but more of a promise.

"But, Mother," Bayle said, panic flitting across her face. "I couldn't stand being locked away. I'd die."

"You should have thought of that before coming here. If you can't control yourself, I'll make sure you spend the rest of your life in a cage."

Locke balled his fists at his side. To hear a parent treat their child in such a manner without an ounce of understanding or love made him physically ill. If he couldn't hear the truth in her words, he'd think she just said these things in the heat of the moment, that she didn't really mean them.

But she meant every word and then some.

She was fully prepared to lock her daughter away for the rest of her existence. Locke realized that this woman had no love for her children, that she most likely didn't even see them as her own flesh and blood. She used them to appease her curiosity, as fodder for her experiments.

He had to rescue Azia from her mother. He had to get her safely away, where this woman could never hurt her.

But instead of grabbing his mate and running, Locke stayed silent, leaning against the wall. As much as he wanted to, he couldn't make such a sweeping decision for Azia. She had to come to this conclusion on her own. It hurt, but he had to stand back and wait. If things went sideways, he would kill Xandra's security guards, they would take the XL4003 and run. For now, he couldn't do anything except watch helplessly.

~

AZIA SAW Bayle fight tears and anger, a strange calm settling over her. She knew her mother wasn't finished with her list of punishments. Not by a long shot. Bayle wasn't the only person who had transgressed.

"Lieutenant, please bring in the others," her mother said, and went back to her notes, leaving Azia purposely in limbo.

Azia breathed in to calm herself, her head filling with the scent of cinnamon. Then she turned and found Locke standing behind her.

He smiled, and everything lightened. She had a mate. She had someone right here behind her that was always on her side, a man who loved her unconditionally. Her heart filled and comfort surrounded her. She might have to leave everything she'd ever known, leave her sisters whom she loved with all her heart, but she would always belong with Locke, safe and cherished. They were a team now. He was counting on her to save him from this situation, so she had to do better than her best.

She nodded her thanks to him. This was a confrontation that had been a long time coming. No longer would she twist herself into a pretzel to please her mother. Those days were over. She needed a backbone pronto, because she had a responsibility to her mate and her unborn children, if she ever had any, to stand up for herself.

There would be no changing her mother. Xandra ElAtal was who she was. Azia knew that now. She would never be the mother Azia had always dreamed of. She had to let those dreams die and move on to the life she wanted, the life filled with love that she deserved.

As she watched her mother working, clearly able to ignore both the pain she'd just inflicted on Bayle and the discomfort she caused Azia by drawing out their confrontation, Azia realized her mother enjoyed hurting them at least to some extent. It was most likely part of the experiment.

The Lieutenant returned with Dru and Caden trailing behind him.

Her sisters appeared the same as they had when she'd last seen them, except for the worried looks on their faces. Caden's short brown hair had a mussed appearance as if she'd been scraping her fingers through it. Dru, on the other hand, had left her straight black hair down, her elfin features making her look fragile, even though Azia knew she was not. Dru had depths she kept hidden while she kept her head down and achieved whatever she set her mind to.

Her mother dropped her pen and refocused on them. "So, Azia, were Dru and Caden involved in this plan to rescue Bayle?"

Excuses wouldn't matter any longer. "They were not," she lied.

Her mother turned to her sisters. "Were you, Dru?" she asked, going to the weakest link of them all.

"I... I didn't know," Dru said weakly, so obviously lying that Azia winced, not even needing her power to see through the words.

"What about you? Were you a part of this?" she asked, shifting her gaze to Caden.

"I wasn't, although I would have if I'd been given the opportunity," Caden said, raising her chin in defiance.

"I see now I made a mistake." Her mother tapped her lips with one long finger. "I obviously changed the experiment by housing you together instead of apart." She picked up her pen and made a note in her notebook.

"If you hadn't let us live together, we wouldn't have flourished. People need human contact," Azia pointed out.

Her mother frowned. "It's true there have been studies that say children die without human contact. I'll have to think about that." She seemed lost in thought for a moment, then refocused on her daughters. "However, you were all aware Bayle had stolen my notebook, yet no one reported it to me."

Azia tried to distract her mother. "The important thing is that Bayle is back with us."

"And you," her mother said, shifting her focus. "You have been very busy since you took an unapproved leave from the Institute."

Azia raised her chin and prepared for battle. "I was trying to save Bayle."

"And you did," her mother said. "Expressly against my orders."

Silence fell as her mother shifted her gaze, finding Locke behind them. "And don't think I don't know about Locke Maynard. The man you broke out of prison." Xandra turned to him. "You'll be going straight back to Hell's Gate by the way, as soon as we come out of jump."

"I'm afraid that's impossible, Mother." Azia forced herself to straighten, keeping her voice modulated and in control.

"Oh? And why is that?"

"He's my mate. If we are too long apart, we'll both die. And that would be the end of your grand experiment."

Her mother blinked in surprise, then huffed out a laugh. "Surely you don't think I'd believe something so ridiculous."

"Believe it or don't, it's true." Azia's first instinct had been to hide her newfound power from her mother but she realized she couldn't do that. She needed to bargain with Xandra for their escape using the one thing her mother wanted above all—data. She took a deep breath. "It turns out your hypothesis about what would trigger my powers was incorrect. I needed a mate to unleash them."

All her mother's focus snapped onto her and Azia

remembered how awful it had been to grow up with this level of observation.

"I find that hard to believe," she said, but Azia had her complete attention now.

Locke stalked to her side. "It isn't something we make public. After all, having a mate might be our biggest strength, but it is also our biggest weakness. Kill my mate and you kill me."

The pen in Xandra's hands dropped onto the workbench. "Mating unlocks Delphi psi abilities. I never considered that. I knew something held back your abilities, but I couldn't unearth how to release them."

"Stress impedes development, not encourages it," Azia said, anger at past treatment stirring. She tamped it down. This wasn't a time to lose her focus and end up airing past grievances.

Her mother seemed to consider that. "Interesting." She made another note in the margin of her notebook. "Next time, I'll add that as part of the protocol."

No, Azia wanted to yell, *no more testing on people, you evil witch!* But she had to save Locke and herself. That was her number one priority. She didn't have the luxury of saving others. *Not yet, but I swear I will in the future. I'm going to dedicate my life to saving people who are in need. From this day forward.*

She didn't know who or how yet, but if—no, *when*—she got free from here, she was going to spend her life helping others.

"What powers do you now possess?" Xandra vibrated with excitement.

I have her hooked. I just need to reel her in. "I won't tell you unless you meet my conditions," Azia said, feeling Locke's gaze on her.

Her mother barked a laugh. "I don't think you're in a position to bargain."

In the past, Azia would have wilted, tried to smooth over, calm the waters, but this wouldn't save Locke, wouldn't save herself. "You're wrong. Because you want very badly to know what powers I possess. And I will not share them unless you agree to my terms. In writing, so you can't renege on a verbal promise."

Her mother face hardened as she sensed her loss of power over Azia. "And what exactly is it you want?"

"First, a pardon for Locke. He has been critical in Bayle's rescue, and he has served this family well. He deserves freedom." Azia channeled every bit of strength she had on this negotiation.

Her mother waved a hand. "What else do you want? I'm growing tired of this back and forth."

Azia wished she'd had longer to plan for this moment because whatever bargain she made with her mother would be binding and impacted all of them. "I will be leaving the Troopers and the Institute, and you will let me go without any interference. Those are my demands."

"If I agree to this, and I'm not sure I will, in return I want a month to explore your powers."

Explore. Azia knew these thirty days would be very unpleasant, but she knew her mother wouldn't agree without having the data she craved. "You may have the return trip through jump to test my powers and nothing you do will physically hurt me, Locke, or my sisters."

Xandra tapped the end of the pen on the counter, thinking.

"This isn't a negotiation, Mother. This is the best deal you will ever get from me." Azia met and held her mother's gaze, turning one of her hands over and lighting her flame so her palm glowed. "Take it or leave it."

Bayle gasped beside her.

The lust for knowledge made her mother's gaze lock onto the glow. She nodded once, slowly. "I'll write up a contract. You will submit your resignation to the Troopers immediately after we sign and will turn over the ship you have been flying. I will no longer support you and you will have no interaction with your sisters from this time forward."

"I will resign and turn over my ship." She had to, since it did not belong to her. "But I will have interaction with my sisters. They are my family and I will not be cut off from them."

"I suppose sending messages back and forth wouldn't be the worst thing" Xandra said. "For now, you will all be placed into observation while I write up the contract."

At her mother's order, they were escorted to an observation room where test subjects were stored, the space too tight for five people, but Azia wasn't going to push her luck by demanding a larger room. Besides, this would allow her to spend time with her sisters. Leaving the Institute meant she would not get to see them often and maybe not for a long time. It would be nice to say goodbye.

"You think she'll stick to the agreement of your terms?" Caden asked as she, Dru, and Bayle sat on a bunk hanging from one wall of the small cell, while Azia sat in the chair nailed in place beside a small table.

"I do." Not surprising her at all, Locke prowled the space, finding a basic bath and empty closet hidden behind the two doors. Keeping her eyes on Locke, she said, "I feel like I'm abandoning all of you."

"Don't worry about me," Bayle said, giving her a look that said her sister was already building a plan of her own.

"Or me," Caden said. "Escape and have a life. You deserve it."

"What powers do you have?" Dru asked, already moving on.

Had Azia known her sisters would want her to go like this, she would have considered leaving long before now. Somewhere along the line, they'd grown up and she hadn't noticed.

Azia smiled at her youngest sister. "Since I'm sure mother is listening to us, you'll have to wait until she signs the contract to hear about them."

Dru's eyes grew huge, and she looked around for the cameras. They seemed to be absent, but there was no way their mother wasn't observing them. They were, after all, experiments.

Locke reached the end of the small room and turned, returned back across the space and finally sat on the table beside her. It groaned under his weight but held him. He leaned down to kiss her cheek. "You kicked ass," he whispered, pride in every word.

"Thanks." She smiled at him, touching his chin because she needed the contact. Immediately, love and need raced over her and she wondered if it would always be like this, always feel so amazing.

He caught her hand and kissed her palm. "Which is good. I wouldn't want to cause strife between us by killing your mother and her security team."

A small laugh bubbled out of her. "That would be terrible," she said, but would it? It would certainly solve so many problems—and cause so many others.

Locke's head jerked up. "You just lied," he said, his eyes sparkling with unreleased laughter.

"Well…" She shrugged, not knowing what else to say on the topic.

He nodded his head once, and she knew he was proud of her, supported her completely. She'd bargained with her mother for their release. A written contract would protect them. And if it didn't, they'd break out and run when they reached the end of jump.

"Thank you for rescuing me," Bayle said. "I know I really messed up this time."

"I love you," Azia said simply, because Bayle always got into trouble. It was her nature. Azia had long ago reached acceptance that this was just the way her sister was. Whomever the Warfran were, she shivered at the thought of a whole planet full of people like Bayle. It must be constant chaos.

She met Locke's gaze again. "My mother will agree to let us go."

He pulled her to her feet. "I know she will. She wants to see what you can do. It proves she was right, that humans can take on alien powers."

"We'll be able to stay in the Interworld." They wouldn't have to run and hide. They could build a life together, settle down and raise their children. Wake up every morning to a house of love and happiness.

"Yes," he said, drawing her into his arms. "Although, I would have been happy anywhere in the universes as long as I was with you."

"As I would have been happy anywhere with you," she said like a vow. "I love you," she whispered into his ear so her mother's hidden camera couldn't see them.

He pressed his lips against her throat, making her shiver. "I love you," he said.

Her heart filled because she heard the truth in his words.

WANT to spend more time with Locke and Azia? Join Leigh's newsletter at www.leighwyndfield.com to access a free epilogue showing where they went next!

Want to read a sneak peak of Bayle's story? Turn the page for the first chapters of Destined coming July 8, 2025!

The End

PSI MATES #2 – DESTINED

CHAPTER ONE

Bayle ElAtal strode down the long, gray hallway of the Institute heading to her rooms, the one place she'd be hidden from vid and could let her guard down. There had been a time in her life when she'd loved this rambling fortress, loved the interesting secrets that waited around every corner, loved watching the soldiers come and go, and the lab workers racing around in their white coats conducting mysterious experiments. As a voyeur, the Institute had been her playground.

But ever since Xandra ElAtal, the Commander of the Institute and her mother, had punished her by sentencing her to a lifetime of being trapped here, the building had become a prison. The walls had closed in on her, crushing her perpetual good mood.

She'd always claimed nothing could bring her down, but lately captivity and constant monitoring annoyed her at best and at worst made her downright—she searched for the right word—something. Maybe depressed? Having never been depressed a day in her life before this, she wasn't sure, but thought the proverbial raincloud that hung over her head could be melancholy.

Adding to her bad mood, the mess hall had been serving a choice of either beef-flavored syn-protein or fish-flavored syn-protein, which wasn't a choice at all. The after-taste of fish in her mouth all day nauseated her, so that was a hard no. For once, she'd like to spontaneously choose what to eat instead of pick from the standard two options. She'd never cooked a meal in her life, but if she did, it would never be fake fish.

Her rooms, which included a small bedroom and a living room, didn't have a food processor, but on impulse she decided she'd requisition one. Since no one, including Bayle, was clear on her status, there was a chance it would be fulfilled. It was time to stop tiptoeing around and push the boundaries of her prison. After all, the worst they could say was no.

She rubbed her upper arm where her mother had installed the tracker, feeling the small square through the sleeve of her sloppy, oversize coat. Even though the injection site had long ago healed over, the piece of metal still burned. As a person who valued her thieving skills above everything, being monitored meant all her adventures had skidded to an abrupt halt.

It was more than the loss of fun or diversion. She *needed* to discharge the pressure. Stealing not only gave her joy, it released the never-ending build of energy that must escape. Like an alcoholic taking that first drink or a marathon runner completing their fifth mile, thieving left her euphoric, but it also allowed her to calm the storm that rose inside her. The need had grown so great, she'd almost stolen a small statue off a display in the mess hall earlier.

She took another left and she entered the small,

attached building where she and her three sisters lived. She, Caden, and Dru still had their rooms here. Their older sister Azia had escaped. Lucky her.

Instead of another empty corridor, Hammond Richards —the bane of her existence—waited outside her door. Over six feet tall, he stood with his arms crossed, his whole body radiating impatience.

Richards was her number one problem, her mother's right hand man and Bayle's personal jailer. A snarl rose up her throat, but she pasted on a blank face instead and pretended she didn't see him. As if that was even a possibility, considering his presence was much bigger than the space his body occupied.

Dressed in his captain's uniform, Richards' black jacket covered a crisp, white uniform shirt, all the buttons done up fastidiously, paired with immaculate black pants and polished-to-a-shine black high boots. The only thing that wasn't fussy were the two blasters, one strapped to each thigh, barely skating the line of uniform regulations. The bureaucrats and scientists of the Institute rarely wore weapons at all, let alone ones slung to their hips. While the butts of the guns were polished to a deep shine, the holsters were battered from long, repetitive wear. It surprised Bayle that her mother let him wear them, especially since it ruined the rest of his pristine, immaculate appearance.

"Your mother requests your presence," he said formally, not meeting her gaze as always, his dark brown eyes dull with annoyance. He tended to stare over her shoulder, his strong, chiseled features pulled into lines that were, in her opinion, filled with censure and judgment. Handsome, she supposed, in a wound-too-tight way. He needed to relax, not that *she* would help with that. She avoided his type like the plague. It was her mother's idea of a joke to assign her such a dud as a keeper. There would be no charming him, no teasing, no fun, no inside jokes with this man.

She ignored him. Her mother had restricted her from leaving the Institute, so she stayed inside the building, but she no longer worked for the Troopers. She'd resigned her commission when she and her sisters had returned from Delphi. It had taken sixty days, but the paperwork had come through. Which meant she no longer had to follow the orders of Hammond Richards.

When she attempted to slide past him, he stepped directly into her path to block her. "Your presence is requested by the Commander, Miss ElAtal," he said, substituting 'miss' for the rank he'd called her up until she'd become a civilian.

Suddenly it was all too much, months of good behavior falling away as impulse drove her to purposely bump into him, slipping her hand into his right uniform jacket pocket. His eyes flashed wide and he jumped backwards, faster on his feet then she would have anticipated. Clear shock from her invasion of his space made his eyes flare wide. She followed him a step to hide sliding the small, metal item she'd stolen into the oversized, sloppy coat she'd started wearing as a protest. Her mother could make her stay here but could no longer force her to look ship-shape and buttoned up.

She almost staggered under the burst of joy that filled her. She'd forgotten that the endorphin release from thieving made her giddy. It had been too long since she'd stolen anything. Way too long. Unable to contain it, she let out a laugh, the sound full of relief. "I don't work for you, the Troopers, or the Institute. My mother can keep me here but she can't force me to attend her."

Bayle chuckled again, unable to tamp down the thrill as

she rubbed the small coin-shaped object in her pocket. It felt like a talisman, still warm from his heat. By not stealing, she'd been suppressing a piece of her she could no longer ignore. When she left here, she could do as she wished, but until then, she had to make peace with who she was to survive.

It hit her like a punch that from now on, she should stop fighting herself and start embracing who she was.

She slapped her palm on the door reader, ignoring the fussy, disappointed "*Miss* ElAtal" behind her and sailed inside her rooms, immediately feeling the comfort of the space as it wrapped around her. She might feel like she was in a prison, but her rooms didn't reflect a jail cell. They were filled with her colorful, messy treasurers.

Reality intruded into her high and some of her pleasure faded as she realized she'd broken one of two rules that her mother had imposed. Xandra had promised to put Bayle in a jail cell if she was caught stealing. Sure, it was partially Richards' fault for placing himself into her path as he had. He'd practically begged her to steal from him when he'd blocked her like he had. But the fact remained that she'd messed up taking something of his. Sadness hit her as she realized she'd have to return the coin before he noticed it was gone.

Behind her the door slid shut only to smack against leather.

Distracted from her self flagellation, she turned.

Hammond Richards' black boot held her door open and his face wasn't full of his usual the polite censure. In fact, he looked pissed. "Your mother requests your presence," he repeated, grinding out the sentence as if he barely held onto his temper. His brown hair was slightly mussed, completely out of character. It softened him and she had the oddest desire to run her fingers through it, just to see what it felt like.

She studied the storm cloud rising on his face, realizing that while he was her personal hell, she must be his as well. She crushed down the spark of sympathy struggling to rise. They both had their crosses to bear.

"Let me put this into small words so you can understand, *Captain*," she said, mimicking his use of her own title. "I resigned from the Troopers. I don't have to follow orders anymore."

The matter closed as far as she was concerned, she spun back to her business, tossing off her jacket with its new prize. She'd explore it later, after Richards had vamoosed from her quarters. Then she'd have to return it. The thought bummed her out more than it should have. For some reason, having something of his appealed to her. Azia would say it was because her moral compass was askew, but Bayle preferred to think it was simply that the concept of ownership had never made sense to her. If she borrowed something that didn't mean she owned it. It was only temporarily in her possession.

Under her jacket, she wore what she'd come to consider her new uniform—an old t-shirt and ancient brown pants with too many pockets. Pockets that could hold all kinds of things...

"I'm afraid this isn't a request," Richards said behind her.

"Go away," she said absently, striding to her bedroom, needing to change and head out to the gym for her afternoon workout, one of the only things she still did religiously. It helped burn off the never-ending buildup of energy. Things had gotten bad lately because she hadn't used her skills. Her mother had been clear that thieving was an offense that would land her in a real prison. While being locked in the Institute wasn't pleasant, as she'd learned from her time on Delphi, a five-by-five cell would be much, much worse.

Xandra hadn't given her a warning when she said she'd put Bayle away—she'd given a promise. Of that Bayle was completely sure.

HAMMOND WANTED to pick up the entitled little priss that was Xandra ElAtal's second oldest child and haul her kicking and screaming over his shoulder to her mother. He had never in his whole life had to deal with such an undisciplined child.

Just looking at her cluttered, messy apartment with random items on every surface and clothes piled on the sofa made his whole body shudder. Almost every inch of the surface of what should have been a dining table was filled with small figurines, a hodgepodge of stuffed animals, people, abstract faces, wooden, ceramic, pottery, the variation making it look like massive chaos to Ham's orderly mind. He resisted the urge to grab a garbage bin and sweep the whole lot into the trash.

Instead, he took a deep breath, held it as he gathered his discipline around him like a cloak, then released the stress in a long exhale. "Let me rephrase. Your mother *ordered* me to bring you and if I need to summon ten men to haul you before her, I will do so."

Usually, he had complete control of his temper, but how long could one soldier babysit? He was, after all, only human. Well, perhaps human was the wrong word, but the sentiment was the same no matter what his DNA might reveal. Sometimes he wondered what he'd done to deserve this punishment.

Wrestling with his temper, he followed her into a small bedroom. He was so pissed it took him a moment to realize he'd entered the inside of a harem tent. The walls were covered in a deep blue fabric, lights winking across the expanse as if he stared into a gorgeous night sky. The bed took up most of the space, pillows piled on top of pillows, the bedding a deep rose. Unlike the first room, this one had no clutter except for an abundance of haphazard, comfortable pillows of varying sizes.

He lost his train of thought for a moment, taking it all in. This was a place for sex, lots of it. Even the smell reminded him of deep loving, earthy, and full of a subtle musk that made him want to bury his face in the bedding and inhale.

He forced his mouth, which had dropped open, to close, shocked at his own imagination. He'd been glued to Bayle ElAtal's side for three hellish months and she'd never even flirted with a man, let alone had one in her apartment. She'd dismantled every bug and camera his team had installed within seconds of returning to her quarters, so he'd never really thought about what her personal space looked like. He had no desire to see how she lived, sending his men in to install the devices. He'd finally given up trying to bug her rooms when she left the camera outside her door, which allowed him to track who came and went. Besides her two younger sisters, in the three months he'd been her babysitter no one else had entered here.

"I guess you're going to have to go get those men then, Captain," she said, not even bothering to turn around as she opened a hidden closet. She freed her blond hair from a messy ponytail, the length flowing down her back in soft waves.

She played with him, a spoiled child having a bit of fun at his expense. He grasped her arm before he realized she'd shrugged off the hideous, baggy shirt she'd worn daily since her resignation from the Troopers. The momentum had her slamming against his chest wearing only a sexy black bra, her shirt still hanging from her other elbow.

They both froze. Her green eyes widened.

Her body, which was usually covered by clothing that appeared rescued from the trash, was all strength, lean muscles stretching on a perfect frame. He'd watched her for months endlessly running, sparring, and training, so on some level he'd known she had to be toned, but he'd been so annoyed by this assignment that he'd made a surface assumption about her and had left it at that. He hadn't gone below the disheveled outer covering. This was a woman who could take care of herself, physically at least.

Unable to look away, his gaze swept down her bare skin. Her breasts were small, but perfectly formed, held lovingly in a black bra that left little to the imagination. Rose nipples peeked through the lace, begging for him to run a finger across the surface to see them tighten. He tried to force his attention elsewhere, but found it impossible.

As if he physically caressed her, her nipples peaked.

Shocking him, every molecule of his body not only approved but ached with need. If anyone had told him he'd have a base level attraction to Bayle ElAtal, he'd have laughed in their face. Just the thought of it jerked him back to reality.

"My apologies," he said, releasing her and stuffing his hands into his jacket pockets since they wanted to return to her flesh again. He ached to run his fingers down her cream and sugar perfect skin.

Her obvious surprise dissolved into a laugh. "Wow, *that*

was awkward, huh Captain?" she asked, her free hand rubbing at the spot he'd touched as if to scrub him away.

Unhappy at the slip of his usually perfect control, Ham reached for his talisman. He dug around in his pocket for a moment but it wasn't where it always rested. Since the coin was attached to a daily ritual blessing, he knew without a doubt he hadn't simply forgotten it this morning.

Xandra had told him her daughter was a thief, but in three months he'd never seen Bayle take anything. He'd been watching her closely, because if he caught her taking so much as a spoon from the mess hall, Bayle would end up in prison and Ham's enforced bullshit duty would be over. For months, he'd wanted to catch her, monitoring her like a hawk, before he'd finally given up. Bayle had been innocent to the point of being so boring he'd fallen asleep on the job. In fact, he'd let his legendary concentration slip and had been sleep-walking over the last month. As time had continued on and nothing had happened, somewhere along the line he'd put his brain in neutral.

Now, he was almost positive she'd taken his coin, the one thing he had left from his people, a talisman he'd been given on his sixteenth birthday to carry with him on this mission. After his planet had been blown to oblivion, the few Warfran left were the ones who had been off-world before the planet had been destroyed in the Forgotten Wars. Xandra's spoiled brat of a child wasn't skipping off with his priceless relic.

While she shrugged into the gray shirt they all wore in the gym, he ignored the pang as her perfect breasts disappeared below the ugly fabric and considered his options. None were ideal. He wanted her to come willingly, wanted her to follow orders, so he could follow his. Xandra had demanded her presence for some reason that might involve

Bayle leaving the Institute, returning Hammond's duties to those of a soldier. But more than anything, he wanted his coin back. That meant he couldn't just turn her over to Xandra and leave it at that. The last thing he wanted was to draw notice to the coin.

Bayle gathered her hair into a messy ponytail.

Leaning a shoulder against the door jamb, he rubbed his eyes so he wouldn't watch her with fascination. How in the fuck had he even gotten this crap assignment? He was a warrior. He fought shit. He didn't sit in a hellhole following the orders of a psychopath like Xandra ElAtal. They called her the Butcher for a reason. A name like that was earned not given.

He tried to remind himself why he was here. Rumors and whispers had told of captured Warfran trapped in the cells of the Institute. If any of his people were here, he would not rest until every single one of them was free. Warfran had special abilities and the hearsay was that the Butcher used them in her experiments. Why, no one knew beyond that she wanted to unlock the secrets of their powers.

After he'd been transferred here, he'd become less sure that was true. In four months, he hadn't seen any indications of his kinsmen. Unlike his own dark brown hair and brown eyes, his people were as a whole tall and blonde. But what made Warfran stand out were their reflexes. Warfran were, compared to humans, astronomically fast. He had to constantly moderate his speed, slowing down so no one would suspect, but in a real fight, he could let his true power shine. He spent his days since his arrival watching everyone, and he hadn't met a single soldier who exhibited the speed of his people. Further, over four months he'd seen exactly two prisoners disappear into the depths of the building and they were clearly not humanoids.

Still... there were secrets here. He could feel them and the one place he knew he'd find the answers was by following the money. He'd sat in on budget meetings, scouring documents but there was no official project involving the Warfran. A little niggling voice in the back of his head reminded him that there had been one line item—210083—which had no official project attached to it. When he'd asked what the item was, no one knew and obviously no one planned to find out. The people he'd questioned advised him to leave it alone. It was the Butcher's personal expense line item. Only she billed to it. He wanted desperately to know what she used the money for, but either no one knew... or no one would tell.

Bayle turned her back and dropped the shabby, bulky pants, bending all the way over, showing a perfect, heart-shaped ass in a black lace thong that matched her bra.

All thoughts of 210083 flew from his mind as his whole body hardened. He suppressed the almost visceral need to cross the room and peel that scrap of lace from her body. His hands shook as he fought a desire so sharp, he took two deep breaths to control it. He had no idea what the hell was going on with this crazy attraction, but it had to stop—now.

He forced every muscle in his body to relax and had a blank look firmly on his face as she turned, giving him an eyeful of her front as she stepped into baggy grey workout pants.

"Enjoying the view?" she asked, without looking up as she pulled the fabric over perfect thighs, hips, and flat stomach.

His mind sluggishly returned to function. "Out of curiosity, do you think I like being assigned to babysit you?"

She blinked, her face filling with surprise before she covered it with a snort. "You'll do whatever you're told to get promoted. All of your kind do."

She breezed past him, her scent curling around to drag him in her wake. Finding one shoe tossed negligently beside the couch, she jammed it on her right foot without bothering to untie it.

He'd never noticed that she smelled of rich spice with an undertone that was slightly sweet, like the Walla bread of his people, the scent so pleasant, he could almost ignore the sight of her tossing random shoes from beneath the sofa in search for the match to the one already on her foot.

If he was attracted to Bayle ElAtal, he obviously needed to find a woman post haste. Any woman. His long time alone had clearly made him insane if he wanted to sleep with this, this—he searched for words to adequately express his feelings—annoying hellcat.

It wasn't as if he'd intentionally chosen to become a monk since he'd been here, he just hadn't trusted anyone who worked at the Institute. The people assigned here kept their heads down and their mouths shut. They answered direct questions, but with an edge of fear if he veered anywhere outside the lines. Every night he took long, blazingly hot showers to rid his body of the foul stench that permeated the air. If he could leave, he'd be gone so fast, Xandra's head would spin. But a higher purpose trapped him here.

One that didn't involve Bayle ElAtal.

"Promotion is not my goal," he said, frustrated at how much this woman got under his skin.

"I find that hard to believe," she said, digging into the pile of crap mounded on her sofa.

It was time to take off the kid gloves and quit jacking

around. "Your mother told me the fastest way for me to get a new assignment was to catch you stealing."

She turned, the other shoe triumphantly held in one hand from where she pulled it from her unfolded laundry heaped on the sofa. "What?"

He made sure she understood exactly what he was threatening. "I have never wanted a new assignment more in my career. To get rid of you would make my fucking year. But try as I could for the last three months, I couldn't find a single thing missing." He walked right into her space and stopped when the shoe in her hand touched his chest. "Until now."

Her eyes, a strange mixture of green and yellow-amber, grew owlishly large, her mouth forming an O.

Good. For once he had control of the situation. "So, here is what we're going to do. You're going to give me back my coin and then come meekly like a good little girl to listen to whatever your mother is going to torture you with." He leaned toward her until his chest pushed the shoe into her now-heaving breast.

Bayle stared at him in shock, for once her constant snappy sass blessedly muzzled.

GET your copy of *Destined* July 8th, 2025! Pre-order on Amazon.com, or sign up for Leigh's newsletter at https://leighwyndfield.com/join-newsletter to for news about the release of the exciting second book in the Psi Mates series and newsletter only epilogues!

ALSO BY LEIGH WYNDFIELD

Can't wait for another Leigh Wyndfield book?

Read on Kindle Unlimited:

Psi Mates:

Chosen

Destined

Intended (coming August 2025)

Fated (coming September 2025)

The Heat Chronicles:

In Heat

Veiled Heat

White Heat

Cold Heat

Desert Heat

Night Heat

Still Heat

Dark Heat

Read wherever you buy your books:

The Bachelor Diaries:

Bachelor on Mars

Bachelor in Space

Bachelor in Atlantis

www.ingramcontent.com/pod-product-compliance
Lightning Source LLC
Chambersburg PA
CBHW051435170626
46809CB00006B/2470